4.95

Turnstiles

Turnstiles

Ursula Holden

London Magazine Editions
1977

For us, there is only the trying.
The rest is not our business.

T. S. ELIOT

SBN 904 388 204

© Ursula Holden 1977

First published in 1977
by London Magazine Editions
30 Thurloe Place
London, S.W.7.

Designed and printed by
The Compton Press Ltd.
The Old Brewery,
Tisbury, Wiltshire.

I

JORDAN slept through the night as if nothing had happened. Ruth knew that he would still be angry when he woke. She listened to him snoring, a rasping on each indrawn breath, then later silence.

'Jordan, Jordan are you awake?'

He wouldn't answer. All night she'd tried to avoid touching him. Even asleep he hated contact with her heavy stomach. It annoyed him. A reminder of responsibility, a reminder of the trap. He brooded; a double-bed was no resolution to rows. He brooded over insults, he brooded over her wifely inadequacies. This time she had gone too far. He'd said that he would never forgive her. His dark eyes had looked at her and hated.

'Jordan, do wake up.'

She slept for half an hour, waking to find the blankets screwed round him, leaving the cold blowing over her. Her goatskin rug was on the floor. The hospital had impressed on her the importance of fresh air. Responsibility started at conception. She minded his selfishness more than she minded the cold. Her hands were numb, the slates on the roof opposite glittered white over the grey. She wanted him to be affectionate.

'Damn it Jordan, you might wake up.'

On the chair under the window was the case to take into hospital. They'd given her a list of requirements, nightdresses, articles for washing. The baby clinic gave her another one for things the child would need when it got home. So many things, so much responsibility. The case was empty but for the two lists. She'd never owned a dressing-gown.

'Oh wake up Jordan.' She'd like to beat him round the ears.

A winter child would be a hardy one; conceived in cold weather, born in cold weather, a winter child would be unlikely to get ill. Once it was born peace would alight. She and Jordan might pull together; advice columns said it could happen.

5

The room was getting light. She heard the scrittering of leaves blowing along the cobblestones, a scrittering like mice. The leaves fell late that year. In Kensington Gardens she'd seen roses, the night frost edging their petals.

'Jordan, don't just lie there.' She felt anxious. Frost in sunlight, leaves falling, were a childhood reminder. She'd been fostered temporarily, years ago. The lady with the walled garden had been Auntie to her. It was the garden she remembered. Her mother used to visit her, walking over the frosted grass of the lawn. The visits were a threat. She'd felt safe in that garden, safe and alone with frost-rimed leaves until her mother came.

She pulled the blankets. He lay like a dead person but he was awake; his eyelids trembled. She felt the old panic. Her mother used to lie awake, incapable of speech, before they took her to the lady with the walled garden. Her mother had liked brandy. Her mother wailed. Both she and her father had appealed to the social worker. Her mother said 'Don't send Ruth away. She's only seven. Things will get better.' Her parents were no match against interrogation, reports, interviews. 'Recommended fostering' had been stamped on forms. Ruth went to the lady with the garden, being happy in the sun there, until her mother visited, walking unsteadily over the grass to her. The last time the fallen leaves had crackled with the frost as her mother spoke to her. 'I tried, Ruth. I tried to make things better. Grab life, don't be pushed around.' She'd dyed her hair a deeper red and tried to talk naturally. She took Ruth back with her. In that garden Ruth started hating her mother. Her father, disabled from the War, had been a museum porter, directing the public to the world's greatest pictures.

'Jordan, I've got a pain. I've started.' If she frightened him, he'd be nice. She did have heartburn. She poked the brown striped poplin on his shoulder. You could imagine pain if you tried. She was in agony.

He swung his legs over to feel for his slippers, saying nothing, not looking at her. He avoided looking below her face now, because pregnant women were like dead fish, ugly. He fitted his slippers, silent, tied his dressing-gown. He rubbed his beard. Last night's anger had given him a sick stomach.

Ruth pulled her hair free from her collar. He would have liked a

6

conventional frilly-nyloned wife. She followed him into the kitchen.

'I've started. I think. What ought I to do?'

'Please Ruth. I've got a stomach ache.'

She smoothed her fringe, still persistent. She wouldn't show defeat. It had been her hair that he'd first loved. He used to pull it, straining her face back up. Loving him contained an element of pain. She put a shawl round her shoulders. He hadn't kissed her for weeks. She supported her stomach with her left hand under her navel. His back was towards her. He moved his hand from his chin, feeling the half inch trim of his beard outlining his jawbone. Its coarseness matched the coarseness of his black hair. He looked like Henry VIII, a bully fingering his beard, not caring for her plight. His stocky build, his beard and look of obduracy were what she'd first noticed. But now he wasn't thinking about her but about his writing. They'd first met at the Institute where she used to work. He studied creative writing one evening a week.

'I'm cold, Jordan. You nicked the blankets, damn it.' He was inhuman, pushing the switch of the heater with a slippered toe. Silence was worse than his abuse. Heat riffed round her ankles. Once he'd groaned with delight over her, her thighs, her thin white body and her hair. She eased her weight from the left to the right foot. Her stomach felt like a battering ram. The battle was ending by her going to lengths to appease. Once it had been her aloofness that he coveted, had lived to have her swaggering body, pulling her head back, raising her to kiss her pointed face and yellow eyes. Now that she relied on him he wouldn't look, had turned from her. His dressing-gown had a pattern of plumed feathers. Her kingly spouse was treating her as redundant before the birth of their child. Which wife of Henry had been small, thin, ginger-haired?

'Talk to me, Jordan.' In the midst of a whine she had to leave him for the bathroom. At seven months she was at the mercy of her bladder, something the hospital dismissed as pressure.

She looked at her face over the basin, baring her teeth, because they stressed the importance of dental care. Her incisors tended to be pointed; a muzzle of a face, with prominent long eyes. He used to call her Ragged Ruth and wait for her on Wednesdays after his writing class, standing with patience outside the life-class where she posed. Now he wouldn't look at her. He'd carried her shopping basket, with fruit in it because of her father being ill, needing those lemon drinks. He'd talked about himself, explained about his poetry, his literary ambition. He said he liked her intellect, gazing at her greedily, suggesting that they go to his flat. She had a good intelligence, he'd said and opened his front door. She brushed her teeth thoroughly, rinsed, spat, brushed again. Love waned as she'd got big. She'd slept with him at once. She heard him fill the kettle. 'If you wait I'll make you breakfast.' He said nothing. She'd set her trap too well. He hated to be tied. 'Three of us for Christmas,' she'd said, and marked mid-December in red pencil on the calendar of English monarchs, putting a circle round Henry's pointed leather shoe. Getting pregnant had been blackmail, getting him to marry her. It all went wrong after the monthly crosses on the calendar stopped and the marriage ring was on. He'd never cared to hear her opinions. She was a good listener, listening came naturally. Once the X's stopped he didn't bother talking. She heard the clink of a spoon.

'Jordan I did say I was sorry. Last night.'

'You've got toothpaste on your lip,' he said, looking glancingly at her, last night's cold hatred still in his eyes. His own lips met the rim of his cup. The hair on his neck quivered as his orange pekoe tea went down. He'd only made one cup. She'd stop begging him. She stared at the orange 'J' on his pocket. She'd stitched it there so happily when she'd first moved in, leaving her father ill and dying to see to his own fruit juices in Battersea. Because she couldn't wait to join Jordan in his mews flat the other side of London. She'd help him. He'd said her looks alone were inspiration. He gave her literary magazines, lectured her about solipsism. He said he wrote sensationally well without the aid of classes. His idol was Gauguin, maker of supreme artistic sacrifice. At this kitchen table he'd mixed drinks the first night. Habitually neat, he'd washed their glasses, explaining that he lived from Wednesday to Wednesday for his class, and to see her, of course. How pleasant that she wasn't as aloof as she looked. She'd been relieved that he'd not heard of her reputation. She'd never been aloof in the way he meant, only aloof inside, was only too pleased to be pushed across the kitchen table to be loved after their drinking. The hard surface had been cold against her buttocks, she'd felt the tickle of his beard. His pale lips pushed her and his hands pinched. Mouths together, the drink in their differing

8

salivas mixed, a warm salivary cocktail. Outside it had been warm. Spring weather. Lips, tongues, hands conjoined, the glasses clinked to the rhythm of their moving. Legs spread-eagled, tink, tinkle, tink, increasing. A glass fell as he moved out of her. Before pulling her skirt down he'd stopped irritably to pick the pieces up. Breakages annoyed him. But he loved her already. He loved her bizarre clothes, bought in the market. He'd call her Ragged Ruth. He poured more drink into the remaining glass. She drank from his whiskered mouth. She poured some into his navel, drank from it. Unusually pleasant he had said. Did she like his flat? She said she'd always loved the market. He told her the peace and quiet of it at night was what he wanted. For his writing. A librarian by day, his writing was his real work, what he'd been born for. It came before anyone. What a pleasant coincidence that she could type. Would she? For him? So she'd moved in at once, conveniently and helpfully into the two-roomed mews flat off the market. Below his was a garage that he leased to his brother Logan. Apart from telling her he never mentioned him. They weren't close, had nothing in common but their shared blood, no contact other than the exchange of rent. With her help Jordan's genius would flower twice as fast. He required her. Because of being needed urgently she hadn't grieved when her father died, had not even felt sad. Throughout the funeral she'd thought of Jordan. It was quite sad, naturally, but there was his will. She'd benefit. And why should Jordan pay rent when she could buy the premises? It was possible, he'd told her. Her father's will would fix it. All hers, including garage. No more financial worry for Jordan. All hers, two rooms and bathroom. The garage rental would be useful too. Enchanting. Leave everything to him, Jordan had said. Then he could leave his library job and write full-time without pressure. They would be comfortable, she could keep on her modelling job. No tears for her father as his death certificate was signed, no tears over the funeral arrangements. She'd looked jubilantly at pictures of coffins, choosing, while inwardly thinking about curtains for the flat. All hers after Jordan fluttered papers. She couldn't be blamed for forgetting her father's face, so long, so grey, so anxious, in favour of Jordan's live dark-bearded one. Her father used to pour porridge from a pan for her, used to worry about money for her deserting mother. Her mother hadn't stayed long in Battersea, after snatching her away from the foster home with the garden. Her father reared her, dying unthanked, forgotten almost instantly. In life he'd worried about Ruth, her clothes, her way of life, had worried that she'd grow up like her mother, bawdy. He'd made her take typing in her last school year, a standby. A woman should have skill, shouldn't depend on her body for survival. Her morals disappointed him. In the sixth form she'd found out what her body could do for her, that kind of survival. With Jordan it was different. The modelling jobs, the living anywhere, with anyone, returning to her father in Battersea between involvements, would change. Quite different now. Really needed. All hers, for Jordan's sake. New start, forget how it was, forget her father, ill, then dead. Forget her mother most of all. She had a real future, her own home, man, own destiny. Her destiny was to help artists. Posing had begun it, showed that she was needed. And Jordan loved her, she was his necessity. There'd been no wedding talk until she'd missed two periods, trapping him on purpose. He'd never wanted that trip to the registry office. The magic dwindled when the ring was on. She started fattening. She couldn't model in that state for long. She'd trapped him purposely, had spoiled the quality of his life, his literary flowering. He'd had to revoke his notice at the library.

'There. Is it gone?' She licked her lips, flicking her thin tongue round.

'Your upper lip.' Jordan hated mess as much as he hated noise and interruption. She'd interrupted his creative work. Because of her it might be years before he saw his book on a library shelf or in a bookshop. Mother bitch. Those X's on the calendar stopped and he'd been robbed. No kitchen table to himself, alone with sheets of foolscap, only the prospect of years more at the library. She'd robbed his solitude. Peace and an empty kitchen had been exchanged for a mother bitch and her increasing size. And the expense. An artist needed space. There wasn't room. Soon they'd be three. As soon as the financial transaction had gone through after the funeral she'd made unpleasing innovations. His Dorset upbringing had taught him to appreciate old furniture, sombre colours, polish. His background must be right for his creating. Once the bitch had power bought by her father's money she changed everything. The ring on her finger was the final straw. 'Out. I like it bare, Jordan. Life should be basic.' He'd come home from his tiresome library to find his bed gone. The mattress lay on bare boards; his Wilton carpeting, his mahogany disposed of. He'd felt quite ill. She'd babbled at him. 'People create a room, not furniture and tasselled curtains.' Hers now, she'd made it plain. Nor was that all. As well as furniture and peace he'd lost clean tidiness for good. She seemed to like dirt and disorder, didn't bath, would rather rub herself with balms. Those once quick-moving bones became lazy. Fish-shaped, slovenly, her typing became careless. The bitch had only kept the kitchen table and the old divan, both too large to take away. He missed his familiar oak bed with nice clean sheets. She expected him to sleep under a disgusting goat skin. He drew the line at that. Last night he'd found mouse-droppings in the frying pan, the print of their claw-marks in the rancid fat. She'd only shrugged, sitting at the kitchen table, lips in a thin bitch smile. She'd been typing his manuscript. She'd crossed through pages of it, red scores of a biro ripping his neat script. He couldn't believe it. She had altered, had ruled out whole paragraphs. He picked up other pages. She had cut with scissors, gluing parts together with her own insertions. He nearly heaved. She'd tampered with his work. One page looked as if she'd spat on it. In margins there were comments. 'Plagiary', 'Keats the morning after', 'Crap.' She'd made a mockery of his own prose-poem. He'd seen then, really seen her true pregnant colour. He'd shouted. Called her 'bitch'. He'd rescued her from living like a tramp, he'd picked her out and married her. For this. This. This. 'By Jordan's Banks I Sighed', was ripped in two. On a folder she'd put 'By Battersea I Puked'. Murderess. She'd shouted back. 'My money bought the roof. I type your opus. Damn it Jordan what do you expect?' It was her typewriter, why was he so serious? She'd been playing about. A joke. He'd said that she was evil. Evil and dirty. Black footmarks on his bedding, jamjars full of old leaves, dirty pans, cushions to sit on, a dirty empty home and this. He picked up the torn title page.

'There. Better?' She licked round again. Teeth were important. Her tongue felt tired from quarrelling. Unwanted, fat, he hadn't called her Ragged Ruth his own true secretary for months. His eyes were enemies. Outside the leaves scrit-scrittered like more mice. Once she'd believed in luck, catching them before they touched ground. Had she ever believed in his work?

'Jordan, we are married don't forget.'

'I intend to forget it. I must have been mad, quite mad to marry *you*.' Anger made his throat tighten. Emotional extremes aggravated his weak stomach. He couldn't forgive her. On top of last night's work she'd made him lose control. He swallowed, forcing his voice quiet. You mustn't be demonstrative, you must show sangfroid no matter what provocation. She'd made him lose dignity. She was unforgiveable.

'But you did marry me. So what will you do about it?'

'You mocked. You interfered. You bitch.'

'I've done a lot for you. The thing of it is, Jordan, your work isn't enough. Damn it, I sit around alone. It may be different after the baby.' She felt glassed in, remote from him. But she had rights, bought by her ring, her state of wifeliness.

'It won't be different. You aren't enough for me. You never have been.' She was inferior. Her hair smelled like an animal. What once had charmed, revolted him. She only washed the feet of his socks, the crutch of knickers, never touched the flat. Her long hair fell into things. Red hair was cheap.

'Isn't it a bit late now?'

'Is it? Your predicament means nothing to me. And you are nothing.' He wouldn't let himself be shamed by her, he spoke firmly and clearly. He had to get away. Downstairs Logan arrived, he heard the sound of the garage door opening. He had ignored him utterly for years. Logan had chosen his own way of living. Jordan would find an alternative to a life with a mother bitch who desecrated his work. The flat had become worse than Devil's Island. He would leave her and her coming child, leave Fyste Close, do what he had to do. Where were his curtains, bed, his nice clean sheets now? Pregnancy and marriage had turned her brain. Nor would he stay with the library. Why should he push inferior books about, list other people's spewings when he could be putting the finishing touches to his own masterpiece? No one understood, his work came before any child. Last night's events proved it. He'd come in, seen her red hair dangling over the typewriter, his vision blurred in a red haze. He'd seen her red scribbling on his pages, known what he must do. He must escape. He'd finish 'Jordan's Banks', follow it quickly by 'Growth in the Green'. His third,

12

'No More' would make the trilogy, all in a row, at eye level, to establish his name firmly in the public mind. No more wasting valuable time, he must forget people, let the world talk as it would. A free spirit, the sooner the royalties flowed the better. That Ruth had chosen pregnancy was her bad luck. Forget her and escape as Gauguin had. He often fancied he heard Gauguin speak, a voice whispering from Tahitian greenery. 'Friend,' it said, 'friend, cut free. I trod this road, cut free and do your work.' What did Ruth matter in comparison? She'd lied to him, far from helping she had hindered. She had ruined his home and interfered. Liar, bitch, cheat. And he'd attended to the formalities for her regarding the house purchase, had sheltered her. She was a disappointment.

'Don't you want me Jordan?'

'No.' Ignore her yellow eyes, her skin that once you'd died to touch, ignore that shiny fringe touching her eyebrows, concentrate on flight. Remember the hair that dropped into the food. Remember your manuscript stinking of oily stuff. Cut free, don't look at her. Below, Logan was moving heavy equipment, before starting work. Ignore him too, cut off, ignore your queasy stomach. Don't look at her.

'Don't forget who paid, Jordan'. She would show fight, she wouldn't walk meekly to the chopping block.

'It will be me that leaves. I'm leaving, do you understand?' In spite of his resolve he shouted at her again. She would madden a saint. Leaving was very inconvenient.

'Go then. Don't think I care. I don't.'

'I'll leave at once.' He swallowed a mouthful of bile. He tightened his dressing gown cord, firmed his shoulders. The whole disturbance had been forced on him; a curse which he'd turn into a blessing. Don't think about your library colleagues who jeered, asked you how the great work was going, and if you were in line for the Nobel. They'd enjoy seeing you made homeless. 'Cut free, friend. Leave.'

'And Jordan, I'll need cash.' Her voice was an echo of her mother's whines. Her earliest memory was of her mother asking her father for more money. But she too must have started on a high note, must have captivated her father, as once Ruth captivated Jordan. Love ended in a whimper for money, a whimper over the same table where love had started. She raised her chin to his neat beard. She used to catch butterflies on the lawn where she'd been fostered, pulled their wings

13

off, watching the bodies crawl. 'Don't harm a helpless creature, dear. You miss your mother,' the garden lady said. She'd gone on catching them, worrying about her mother coming again. The insect bodies crawled lop-sidedly. She wondered if he remembered the first night, the table top, the night sounds. The tap had dripped, a sound of eastern pipe music sounded in the market, the glasses clinked accompaniment. Zips, buttons, fasteners clicked against the table top. 'You understand my work is vital. It has priority.' 'Oh I do. I'll do your typing.' The next morning she had woken by him in his solid bed, had seen a branch outside the window, unfurling green buds, a greenish mist in the light, like a beginning. Their beginning was ending in a cry for cash. How long did those butterflies last?

'I don't intend to leave you destitute.' He had his pride. 'Be haughty friend, don't weaken.'

'Sod off.' Her mother's coarseness in her mouth. Her mother who'd been an evacuee, affected by wartime childhood, like damaged goods, resulting in an adult taste for the whoopee lasting into middle age. Her mother who never took life as it came but wanted something better. Had wanted a better life than Battersea, had turned to brandy, got hooked, ruled by her craving. Her mother ruined her childhood, split the family.

Jordan left the kitchen. The worst was over, he wouldn't go back now, could leave with his dignity. As boys in Dorset Logan and he'd caught insects. Logan was tender hearted then. The bruised-winged ones had to be killed the same as the perfect ones, he wouldn't release them to take their chance. Goodbye past times, goodbye Logan, goodbye mother bitch. He'd find alternative quarters. The junior assistant with the wet lips in the library might type for him. Somewhere, someone else, peace, a pleasant life again. Ruth had a filthy tongue. Flat-hunting was so time-consuming.

'Sod off. Thanks for nothing.' She licked her lips again. She hadn't cried for her father, had only licked her thin lips as they pushed a button, making his body slide from sight. She was a part of him. They were burning him. She'd licked and concentrated on Jordan, on moving to the flat, on Wills and Testaments and being needed. Afterwards, as they'd left the crematorium, she'd seen a figure at the gate, too late for the ceremony, a swaying figure with untidy ink red hair, flowers in her hand. Her brandy-sodden mother missed the function.

14

Ruth felt no compassion, had ignored her and her broken-stalked flowers, ignored the note received next day. 'Your father didn't understand. It wasn't my fault. I shall miss his money.' She'd put her out of mind, put her dead father out of mind, in the joy of putting signatures to papers. As if the sad figure pouring porridge for her had never been. As if her mother's high heels, ink-red hair and awful face had never been. Her own home, she would fly.

'I won't be back. Don't think I will. I won't.' He felt his face get hot under his beard. A beard protected you. An artist needed conceal-ment. Sensitive, ill-used, unappreciated, he was hellishly inconveni-enced. You had to pay the price. Relationships were only valuable if they served art. Ruth and he weren't complementary. He'd write alone, or with that wet-lipped junior. He felt the ghostly hand stretch from a far green jungle, patting him. 'Well done friend.'

'Sod off.'

2

OWNING a place didn't give you safety, nor did pregnancy and marriage. What she most feared had occurred again. The fear of being
jacked in. Her monarch was going. Too late to wish she hadn't
shouted. She hoped his brother Logan hadn't heard. The garden lady
had been courteous, rating right conduct highly. Her mother screamed
'Sod off', gulped aspirins on her mornings after, before whining to her
father about money. Her father went on trying to run the home quietly, despite drunken disorder. He'd thought Ruth should stay with the
garden lady, lit by peace and right example. Instead her mother,
weaving on high heels, came and got her back, persuading the authori-
ties. The garden lady kissed her. Life was what you made it. Affec-
tion mattered, honour. Young though she was, she had confidence in
Ruth. Back in Battersea it was the same. Her mother went on crying
into torn paper hankies, farted in the armchair having stayed late in
the West end. There were ways of getting money, ways that eventually took her from Battersea for good, a permanent whoopee after
her final words to Ruth. 'Make a good thing better.' Jordan had no
interest in her background. Only his future mattered. A pity that his
final memory of her would be a vulgar shout. A pity that she'd spat.
    Coathangers clicked along the rail she'd put in the corner instead
of his heavy cupboard. Shoes thumped. A further thump of library
books. 'Jordan, you cannot do it. You can't put books and your own
pride before me. People come before prose-poems. Don't.'
    Outside the leaves continued. Goodbye, the death-dry sound of
leaving. Now he was in the bathroom, having bolted the door, a man
for privacy to the end. Physical signs, the body's leavings disgusted
him. The X's on the calendar of monarchs disgusted him; a woman's
cycle should be unmentioned. Worst of all was when the X's stopped.
He'd tried to alter her, to make her use deodorants, wash more. The
sight of an unflushed pan upset his digestion, she'd spurred his leavetaking by her sluttish ways. He was still a stranger to her, marriage

16

didn't bring closeness, she still knew nothing of his Dorset child-hood. Like Logan he had been to grammar school, the only two in his family with scholastic ambition; he'd shown no interest in her own background, except to criticise her accent. He fussed about her vowels. The way you spoke could impede or speed promotion in lib-rarian circles. Now he would forget his promotion, follow his phoney star and she could forget his standards. She would eat as she wanted. No more bleeding steak to feed his poet's brain, but brown rice, well-seasoned. She'd use the rue, the tansy, the tarragon in the wall rack and write openly in her diary. Don't go Jordan.

When he came out of the bedroom wearing his overcoat he carried the case for the hospital. She knew then. It was final and she'd never again rush to him, to push her face, her tongue, hands into him. Jor-dan Cash A.L.A. could not accept her as she was. His whim, she'd overstepped the mark. She had avoided grieving for her father eleven months ago, she would avoid grieving now. In order to avoid grief she'd grabbed Jordan. 'My father is going to die' she'd told him, there by the table. 'Don't be sad, I'm here. What are your typing speeds?' Instead of grief she'd taken wing. He'd remembered to repeat often that he loved her desperately until she changed the flat. A game, to the beloved you were parent, cook, lover or typist, paying the price when love died. Game over. She wouldn't cry. She could put her diary on the table openly. She'd be herself. Don't go, don't go. The butter-flies had been cabbage whites, bright in the sun. The garden lady said that all creatures should be treated equally, with kindness. Destruc-tion, discrimination achieved nothing. She'd learned not to cry on that lawn. You learned control when you found you couldn't con-trol circumstance.

Jordan looked at her for the last time. The corner of the table dug into her stomach. Her hair hung round her face. She didn't look up again. He felt relieved of a great burden, the burden of having changed Ruth Brown into Ruth Cash was being put aside. The stair-rail rat-tled as he descended. The building was old, needing repair. Loose parts would grow looser, more plaster would crumble from behind the cooker. Let her stay, do what she liked with it. The price of freedom was a high one. He wished, though, that she didn't wring her hands like that. He banged the door, not noticing the frost, the leaves, not noticing Logan, head under the bonnet of a car. He needed only to put distance between himself and his wife and brother in Fyste Close, a place of tumbling buildings, storage lofts and garages. I shall be lonely. I have no regrets. 'Friend, well done.'

She didn't move. She wouldn't go to the window to watch him. This was how corpses felt; dry-eyed, sorry for a finished life, reluctant to enter the next. His feet made little noise receding. From the guttering across the Close dead weeds stuck up like bones. In spring the sparrows nested in the broken brickwork. That first morning she'd seen nestlings on the cobbles, dead under the unfurling buds of the plane tree. It had been blue and warm. Now, game over, dead-dry, white and finished, she had another life inside her. She was cold, old. Her planning hadn't paid. She'd started planning from the start, as soon as she had seen the flat, had planned how she would alter it. While posing at the Institute, while watching her father's body slide away she'd planned curtains, window boxes, a clean sweep of his furniture.

She'd put ice plants in the boxes on the window sills outside. Their pink clusters were withered to brown dryness now, the leaves settling there in patches.

A stalk tapped the window. Noises, outside life continued, leaves scrittering, the clinks and bangs of Logan, the early shouting in the market as stallholders put up their trestles, unloaded their wares from vans with squeaking brakes, or pushed their carts with heavy metal wheels. Jordan would notice none of this, treading his higher plane away from her. Their interlude was over. She'd known it wouldn't last. Inside, she'd known. She knew too that winged things could survive, birds, damaged flies. Torn, isolated people learned to manage. Logan would have to be told.

She lay down in the cold imprint of Jordan's body. No sign that he'd lain there. She sniffed his pillow; no snippings from his beard, no indicant. A bed should respond, a bed should retain evidence. Crumbs, scraps from condom packets, stains, hair from genitalia, signs that two had loved. There was nothing. No skin-flakes, odour, nail or nose-pickings. Jordan complained if an eyelash fell onto the soap. He'd found a hair along the fat of his steak and shouted. 'Couldn't she control the stuff, wrap it in a scarf, be cleaner?' He'd taken all the library books. How did you get an affiliation order?

She was by the telephone in the kitchen before three rings had sounded.

'Jordan? Is that you Jordan?'

'Jordan? At this hour? Has he left for work?'

'Oh. Primrose.'

'Whatever's wrong? A trifle fraught, aren't you?'

'Jordan's gone. He's left.'

Telling Primrose, saying it out loud confirmed the finality. She knew that Primrose would secretly be glad. She wouldn't say 'I told you' but she'd smile at her end of the telephone. Before her own marriage, Primrose had been a secretary at the Institute. She too, had put her Battersea past behind her, intent on bettering her life. Primrose hadn't believed in loving casually, but believed in saving herself. She'd kept her body as a bait, collateral for the future. A woman had a price. Primrose's price was seven thousand a year, rising with inflation, for life. She'd felt contempt for Ruth living profligately, while envying her looks and ability to beguile. She'd gloated each time an affair broke up, gloating and waiting, saving her own virginity for her successful osteopath who loved, with seven thousand and increasing prospects, for life. As Mrs. Primrose Pownde-Welling she need envy no one. Her saving had bought interest as fine as gilt-edged investments. She could feel a glow of patronage now.

'You're sure? Not just a mood?' She'd never trusted him and his silly writing. Jordan should stick to his profession, quite credit-worthy, with scope for promotion, if not as remunerative as osteopathy. How she'd changed from the days of envying Ruth, pinching boyfriends' sweaters, trailing the passages of the Institute in odd clothes, attracting male eyes with or without them. Ruth used to make her feel so tall and fat. Her chastity had never been bombarded. She'd had to knit her own sweaters. She used to like the gossip. Ruth was called 'slut' and 'pushover' by rivals, and her bright hair, bones and slitty eyes had brought her little. She'd evidently been ditched, was talking into the telephone in a frantic way.

'He's often moody, I was used to that. The thing of it is, Primrose, he's left me.'

Both from Battersea, both wanting better lives, Primrose had hers in her hand. With her father a grocer, her weight had been acquired early. To wean his interest over to her she'd tried to eat his stock up, failing. At almost six feet high, enormous head and hands, she'd

19

laid her plans early. She'd saved her wages for a course in charm. She hadn't dieted, but learned the social arts, how to conduct herself in public places, above all how to speak. Behaviour mattered more than looks. Miss Chips of Charm Enterprises had made a lady of her. With her car, credit cards and household staff in Weybridge she had status. Pete wouldn't stray and her large hands would never type again. They tightened now about her pink telephone, tightened with excitement at the news.

'Well, I rather thought so, Ruth. I am sorry.' Librarian he might be, writer possibly, staunch provider, no. He talked a lot. Where was the fruit? Nothing in hardback. Ruth had been feckless to pitch her inheritance into a rundown slum house, sillier to marry and get pregnant. Talent must show a profit. She'd spoiled her life. Thank heavens for the name of Pownde-Welling, the only one in the directory. No use pining, Ruth must look again. Jordan had proved twopenny, she must go where money lurked, the Young Conservatives, or a pottery class. Thank heavens for Miss Chips.

'Can you come over, Prim?'

'Well . . . when I've done the ordering.' Her first loyalty was to her household. She only hoped their break-up was clean and lasting. Ruth must outgrow the habit of hand-wringing over the past. She ought to save.

Hard-skinned, Ruth's hands went scaly in cold weather. Dirt stayed in the cracks. The garden lady had said value what you had, turn it to advantage. Her hands embarrassed her, a reason for avoiding water. A natural slob, she'd rather in any case stuff dishes under the divan than wash. She put some plates there. She'd do her face for Primrose, dusting it with green-toned powder. She painted her eyesockets, extending her brows like antennae to tilt up to her fringe. She got out her velvet smock. Bought to please Jordan, he had never seen it, had never seen her wear brown, soft and conventional. Her other clothes, shawls, saris, oriental things hung from nails on various walls like raggy pictures. She rubbed wood oil into her fingers as Primrose turned into the Close. Her engine was quieter than the blowing leaves. The bell went.

'Barefoot, Ruth? On those bare boards? A trifle rash.'

She wore a sheepskin coat over her cashmere trousers. Pale colours increased her size. She no longer cared about hugeness as she looked with small blue eyes at Ruth, wanting the story at once. She was as big as a sheep.

'I told you. He has gone.'

'Tell me the details, Ruth.' Being fat was rather laborious at times. It made you pant up stairs. Ruth's stomach was quite large. Primrose was fond of the letter pages of magazines that dealt with the pain of severed relationships. She wanted to hear about the downfall, though she couldn't spare long, because of lunch and Pete liking his food.

Ruth explained about the altered manuscript, the shouts and the leavetaking. She didn't say she'd spat or sworn. Her stomach at its largest point was about the size of Primrose's waist. She remembered Primrose's father at his grocers' till, opening and shutting it with the fascination that Primrose showed now, the greed of acquisition.

'Then what happened?' She looked at the filthy floor, the fat-splashed kettle, oddments of clothing on the wall. A man needed a tidy, welcoming home. To keep his love you had to keep the bargain. What had Ruth done for Jordan? She knew the fridge would be unspeakable inside. Under the draining board was a broken packet of rice, tea, a heel of some bread. The only unneglected sight was Ruth and that rather pretty herb-rack. Weeds in jamjars were objectionable. Primrose spoke carefully as Miss Chips had taught her.

'Have you any money? For your immediate needs?' Ruth said she had two pounds. She looked vaguely at Jordan's hateful tea. How condescending Primrose was. Jordan might have left some books.

'He hasn't really done a lot for you.' Two pounds and an empty fridge was a trifle below the mark. Ruth must get those dry hands on someone more lucrative. She could see the kind of letter Ruth's plight would make, and the answer 'Go to your nearest Welfare Branch. Don't be down-trodden.' She wouldn't act as Ruth's welfare officer.

'I believed in his writing at first.' A falsity, like him. She fiddled her fingers, her anger gone. She felt weak and anxious, wishing she had learned to knit instead of sleeping with so many men.

'That's rather a charming smock. Not your usual colour. Did the buttons come on it?'

'They were on a doll. I liked the buttons.'

It had come from the Emporium in the market, a place of junk and pseudo-antique things. The owner was a friend, had given Ruth the doll, had said it was an heirloom and would bring luck for Ruth's future. She'd cut the buttons, the size of tenpenny pieces enamelled with fruit, for her brown smock.

'A doll? An old one? I'd rather like to see it' Victorian ones were often valuable.

Ruth said she'd put it away, the doll gave her the creeps.

'Where? I must see it.'

Ruth got down on her knees. She felt Primrose watching as her stomach touched the floor, watching her root under the valance among the dirty dishes, shoes, toast crusts and old hankies.

Primrose held the doll at arm's length. 'It smells. You're right. It's rotten.'

Its clothes were frayed, the lace round the bonnet worn to threads. Only the eyes in the cracked mask were undamaged, cold and staring. The hands waggled from its leather arms, the stumps of its feet trickled sawdust. Primrose said she'd heard of coins, jewelry hidden in old toys. She tipped it upside down and shook. A lock of hair fell, then the bonnet, Slowly the head left the neck in a widening slit, dropping to the floor followed by more sawdust. No money, only the silent trickle of sawdust. Hair stuck to the bonnet on the floor. Primrose grimaced. You could get germs from refuse. Ruth said she couldn't throw it out for fear of hurting her friend's feelings. Everybody in the market knew her, the Lady Podesta Doge, owner occupier of the Emporium, sensitive person, kind and well thought-of. She re-wrapped the brown paper over the head and body. Its buttons had been useful.

Primrose said she must come to Weybridge one weekend. She wiped her hands on her sheepskin pockets.

3

SHE'D never waited for the telephone before. She used to pity Primrose in the past, waiting vainly for its ringing. Now she knew how it felt. She checked the dialling tone. Might Jordan have tried while she'd been checking? She asked the operator for a test call, begging 'hurry, do'. She had to know how she'd survive. She was too proud to ask for official help. Her two pounds were gone.

She told Logan, leaving the street door open, ready to run up at the first tinkle. He'd looked at her, concerned, he hadn't seemed surprised. He'd not asked questions . . . A quiet man, they'd barely spoken, apart from 'hello'. Jordan hadn't wished them to meet. Chalk and cheese, with nothing to unite them but their boyhood past. Leasing the garage to Logan was financially convenient. Brotherly attachment was dead. So Logan was mysterious, a person who made strange noises down below, mending machinery by day, an artist in his free time. At night he stayed late, sculpting. When she told him about Jordan he stood still, his hand on the car bonnet. He was much taller than Jordan, fair, clean-shaven. She mustn't get depressed, he said. He was there if she needed anything, anything at all. She only half heeded him, because of missing the telephone.

She watched for the postman. A letter came at last, with a Littlewoods Pools envelope, the two falling with a gust of cold through the letter flap. The envelope felt cold. Ruth Cash, 3 Fyste Close, in large librarian script. She picked at the sealed edge, wishing she had the strength to scribble 'Rot' over it, mark it 'return to sender'. Her world had shrunk to hoping and waiting for words by telephone or post. Inside was a cheque for three hundred pounds, wrapped in a book order-form. He had written on the back 'What I said still stands. Ever Jordan'. The form was an inter-borough request for *By Grand Central Station I Sat Down and Wept*. It was his reserve money, money to fall back on after leaving the library, before the royalties started. He'd have no deposit now, for somewhere else to live. The garden lady had tried for a short time to teach her to play the violin, to surprise her mother with her favourite tune. Ruth hadn't grasped the rudiments, a wail or squeak at best. She and Jordan had danced together that first time to the tune, there by the table having drunk and loved, their bodies making one shape in the dark lit by the pilot of the water heater. Glass splinters pricked her feet. 'You'd be So Nice To Come Home To.' Jordan had no home, nobody to come home to. She had his injunction by the crumbs and teacups. Her scruffiness and interference had lost him.

When Primrose rang she didn't tell her about the cheque. Primrose and Pete thought Ruth was being a trifle foolish. There were ways of tracing people. Sting Jordan, go to a lawyer. Ruth had been foolish not to have had a proper wedding, with gifts of clocks and toasters, insurance against a broken future. She would collect Ruth later, take her back to Weybridge. When she arrived she bought a gift of steak, the blood seeping round the folds of plastic covering.

'Can't you let this place? Find somewhere less seedy? Don't the market people depress you? Riffraff. You have no friends.'

Ruth said she had friends. Logan downstairs if she needed him. She had the Doge in her Emporium.

'Him? Your brother-in-law?' It was to be hoped he'd be Ruth's ex-relative very quickly. A greaser. Another loser, doing repair jobs, wasting time making peculiar objects. Had Ruth seen a lawyer? That Doge person was weird, best kept away from. Was Ruth going loco?

'I'm not going to chase Jordan. Logan is kind.' She told Primrose about the cheque. Friendship didn't depend on words. Logan had a reputation in the market for reliable repairing. Old fridges, bikes, heaters as well as cars, found their way to him and sometimes these were never collected. Because of that he'd started sculpting, making ready-mades from unpaid repairs. Sculpture became his real love. When his garage was closed you knew he was working on a construction made from spare parts. Occasionally he sold small mobiles to the Doge for her Emporium, to tempt visiting Americans in summer. The larger pieces were stored at the back of his garage in the corners. He kept to himself, at the same time he was interested in everyone. Unlike Jordan he was liked. He was a good listener.

'Greaser. He won't amount to anything. If only Jordan had stuck to his job.' Both brothers appeared to have delusions. A borough

24

librarian was a worthwhile position. To dabble in literature or art was profitless, Ruth should avoid such people. Like the working-class, anyone without a profession should be avoided. Artists were impractical. Saving came first. Ruth should avoid anyone who spoke badly, aspired to write or paint. Both of them had seedy Battersea pasts to live down. Primrose still winced if she entered a grocer's shop. A navy apron, a pair of bacony hands over a till repulsed her. Now she had Mrs. Pluto, her housekeeper. Miss Chips had done her work, she spoke as well as anyone. Ruth would be getting romantic ideas about the greaser next. Semi-skilled plus arty aspirations, he'd be the kiss of death. As Mrs. Pownde-Welling she was equal to Royalty.

'I have other friends.' A friend was an intimate acquaintance, well-wisher, favourably disposed. The stall-holders in the market knew her as the friendly wife of that library chap, the stuck-up cold-eyed one, not like his brother Logan. Primrose didn't understand. You got used to places, they meant as much as people . . . She'd always liked the market. Now, pregnant, leaving was unthinkable.

Because of Logan, Jordan's face was already blurred a little. She could remember single features, the pale lips cupping his mug, his hating eyes. Her skin remembered his hands, stroking, exploringly at first, strokes that became automatic, then half-bored, a routine stroking of the fingers that soon preferred gripping his pen to gripping her. She had the home, why move? Jordan had pinching fingers, that pulled her hairs as though he sometimes hated her body. Her account of her childhood, her runaway mother, her fear of disaster bored him. She would throw that steak away. Jordan had been the meat-eater.

'Come on then, Ruth.' The girl must stop rubbing her hands and come to Weybridge, warmth and sanity. Primrose wished she'd dress conventionally. Trailing shawls weren't right for Weybridge. She told her not to pack anything. She'd lend Ruth a nightdress.

'I'll tell Logan where I'm going.' You felt safer if someone knew, if your leavetakings were noted. Logan smiled. He was working on a Rolls that he planned to keep. Bought after an accident, he'd been repairing it for weeks. Now it stood outside his doors, proud on the cobblestones. He leaned against the window-frame, listening with interested kind eyes. He'd keep an eye on the flat, she could give him the key. She would benefit by a change. Ruth felt ashamed of Primrose, who turned her head rather than acknowledge him. But Logan went on smiling with rather full lips that balanced his long-lobed ears. He bore no grudge against Primrose, who was befriending Ruth. He'd clean her windows for her. He hated being idle. He lived unhappily with someone in Ladbroke Grove, Jordan had told Ruth. Jordan's face used to tighten with annoyance at mentioning Logan. His fine straight hair was parted. He had thick eyebrows, a feather-stitching over his grey eyes. He'd never pried, was happy that Ruth was feeling better and going away for a weekend. He had to stoop under his garage doors. His stone-coloured eyes weren't hard, creasing at the corners as he raised his arms in a prophet's gesture. When his face was serious his eyes stayed warm.

Primrose said, before she started her car, how much she disliked his type, unskilled and living on his wits. Con man, greaser, smelling of diesel oil. She hated the way he looked at Ruth, it wasn't fair; pregnant, ill-looking, abandoned, she still effected that switched-on awareness in men's eyes.

'You oughtn't to be snooty, Prim.' Logan had skills, talent and humanity. Unlike Jordan her stomach seemed to inspire him. Though they had spoken little she'd not met anyone like him. His constructions were unlike anything she'd seen, though he preferred not to talk about his art. Jordan's work lacked truth. Logan preferred to deprecate rather than boast. Jordan was a spiritual catastrophe.

'I'm merely particular who I associate with. It's done me no harm has it? Rather the reverse.'

'Will Pete mind me coming?'

'He wants what I want.' Primrose's voice was law in Weybridge. Natural ruler, she had her own investments, broker, her personal allowance fixed before the honeymoon. She glowed with affluence. Peter lived to please her. She thanked Miss Chips for her business sense. New cars each year, holidays, home improvements were taken for granted in Weybridge. Capitalism mattered. She'd seen Ruth's sink. A kitchen sink indicated character. Ruth's sink was that of a loser. Her own large size, yellow curls, ambition had got her Pete and security. It enraged her that she could ever have felt envy for someone so small, bony, redhaired and with a child inside.

26

Pete was enormous. He had to be huge enough for massaging the most wayward patients. Ill persons respected size in an osteopath, he believed. He was in the Weybridge kitchen fitting dishes into the new dishwasher. He'd rob the Crown Jewels for Primrose, who was being wonderful to her poor young friend, fishing her from a slummy market-place. Her plight was the very devil. He was quite willing to help, though victims tended to make him rather impatient. It all seemed unnecessary, the bother and the gloom, when forethought could have prevented it. Had he been consulted he might have arranged something, though abortion was not his stamping ground. He thanked heavens for Primrose, so large and bustling in his home. She sounded like the Queen. He wouldn't swap the Koh-i-noor for her. He'd had electric curtain pulls fixed round their bed, to draw open at a touch.

'Primrose wanted you here. You like that idea, Ruthie?' His fingers teased her elbow. Touching parts of patients with undertones of sexiness was a secret he'd learned early. He coaxed pained muscles to retract or loosen, coaxed tension, fears away, his puffy-lidded eyes glinting from behind his spectacles. He coaxed lady sufferers into feeling needed, and gentlemen as well. His bank manager smiled at him. He thought the world of Prim, giving her services ex gratia to Ruth. Shops and firms competed to do business with the Pownde-Wellings. He had a secret yearning to be Chancellor of the Exchequer. He didn't believe in handouts for the down-trodden, but Ruth, small-boned as a squirrel, brought out the paternal in him. Poor little creature. She'd gone and believed something nonsensical about her husband's writing, some library fellow. Now in the club, she'd been ditched. She'd had rather a sexy past, posing nude for artists. Poor squirrel, instead of feathering her nest, she'd landed in the cold. She did have some kind of roof, true. He rubbed and petted her. He asked where she'd booked for the birth. He'd like to look her over, check her muscle tone. He asked to see her tongue, observed how long and pink it was, a nice thin sexy tongue. She wasn't big. Quality of muscle could make the difference between an easy and a tricky birth. A toothsome squirrel.

'I'm only staying one night,' she said quickly. As soon as she'd arrived she wanted to get back. His crawling hands, the hot rooms, the satin nightdress edged with swansdown lent by Primrose made her desperate. She tried to edge from the bump of Peter's genitals, discrete under his cashmere suiting. His after-shave smelled clinical. He wore tussore shirts.

'Ruth. Oh Ruthie, stay,' he said through wetted lips. He could see her ribcage above her belly. Her long hair, shiny fringe were really yummy. He'd like to see her at his table for a long, long time, eating Primrose's lovely food. Food was a manifestation of love. Primrose kept the finest table in the Home Counties. How much and what you ate were a measure of success. It all went back to those yummy school tuck-boxes of his. Primrose had taken over where his mother left off. He'd like some of the largesse to go to Ruth, poor squirrel. A bother, getting in the club.

'I must get back. I have to.' Away from the gold-rimmed glasses, set like horns under the bald head, away from the huge hands feeling her. The ram was offering her a room in his pen. Food, heat, comfort in exchange for pinching her expectantly.

'Why Ruthie, why?'

'The thing of it is, my friend expects me. She has a cat.' She babbled in embarrassment. The Doge was troubled by rats. They hung about the market, scavenging, bothering the Doge, whose cat did little about them. All she wanted now was to get back.

'A cat, Ruthie?' Pete's fingers gave a tremor. He hated animals. Pets were abominable. Prone to veterinary ailments, they brought trouble. No wonder Ruth was tense, worrying herself with cats and arty notions. He wouldn't have one near him. The little woodland creature under his hand was different, she was toothsome. Why concern herself with such problems? Tension could cause maladjustment and no end of trouble later. Cats were the very devil. He stroked her rough hands tenderly. He kept his own smooth with glymiel jelly. She must forget cats, market riffraff, concentrate on him. He'd show her how.

Primrose called from the dining room. The home was furnished plentifully, ornamental cabinets, cut glass in abundance, electrically mechanised objects. There was every kind of drink.

'No brandy, thanks,' Ruth said. It would always remind her of her mother, breathing remorse and brandy fumes over her in the small hours. Pete shook his large head sorrowingly. Ruth ate so little. She'd not touched Primrose's steak or delicious mousse. Fancy playing about with mousse.

'A drink would buck you up, Ruth.' Primrose had done her best. She thought that she deserved to be emaciated. Her kitchen was her temple, she trusted no one with the cooking. With switches to motivate spit-roasters, air conditioners, timing clocks, blenders, she moved like a priestess. Her deep-freeze was formidable. Ample size kept pace with ample appetite. Ruth had stared at her lunch as though it were rat poison.

One night was plenty. Ruth said she ought to be near home, near the hospital, in case. She missed her rusty stove, lit by matches, missed her mobiles hanging from the light bulb, missed burning joss sticks and her goat skin. Mice didn't matter if the atmosphere was right. She felt disjoined in Weybridge. She watched Primrose chuck her body against Peter to be fondled. Primrose wanted no confusion. Pete was hers. The lighting shone on her pale hair. The decor echoed her pink and yellow colouring, she dressed in pink and yellow. A firm called 'Thoughtfully' arranged her flowers, men from an agency – 'Nicer Nooks' – came three times a week to clean. She had Mrs. Pluto for the rough. Pink and yellow roses reared from shelves and tables. There were no books. Ruth had been put in the third spare-room.

'What are you writing, Ruth? I've brought you a milk drink.'

'Just my diary.' She covered it with Primrose's satin-edged blanket. A diary to put words into each day was necessary to her. Recording the doings of her life gave it purpose. She liked to lie in bed and scribble, tried to avoid entries such as 'got up. Miserable. Forget what I did.', tried to avoid mentioning weather, money or boredom. What counted was how you really felt, about people, about what happened. From a practical viewpoint a life could depend on a diary. You might have to give court evidence. The day the cheque came she'd put 'Jordan isn't coming back. I put away my typewriter.'

Primrose said that diary-keeping was a morbid thing, especially just now. Ruth knew it was useless to try and explain. The future depended on how the past affected you. Past, present, future became one in a diary.

'Drink this before you sleep.'

'I can't drink milk, remember, Primrose?'

'In your condition I think you should.' She'd stirred Horlicks into it. How ungrateful Ruth was.

Ruth poured it into the yellow bidet. The bathroom, arranged with 'Thoughtfully' flowers, the chromium fittings, heat, were worse than a coffin. She hoped Primrose wouldn't give her any bacon. Milk, meat, sweet things revolted her. The clock moved silently. In Fyste Close, Logan would be working at one of his metal constructions. To think of him consoled her. In his own way Peter was as dreadful as Jordan.

'Best gammon, Ruth. I scrambled the eggs, in case fried ones didn't agree.' She had arranged the breakfast prettily, a pink and yellow spread for Ruth's thin knees. She felt magnanimous, knowing that Ruth was going soon. She could afford to pamper her. It had been a mistake to ask her. Ruth had an appalling life; she'd brought it on herself. She'd lost no time in getting Peter's sympathy, had cashed in on her poverty-stricken, ill-fated situation. Primrose had seen her making up to him, pushing that stomach into him. To think she could have been jealous. Ruth was no better than a tart. Kind Peter would help any stray. She regretted lending her a nightie, she didn't like her scent. How dare she ogle Pete. Chain anklets were a sign. Her toes weren't clean. Tarts got money regardless, kept quiet about it. Thank heavens she was going of her own accord. She and Pete never spoke about a child. Their Weybridge world was perfect as it was. She was glad she'd given Ruth no money.

The taste of the grapefruit was welcome to Ruth. The smell of bacon, roses, orange pekoe tea was overpowering. Primrose watched her lick the spoon. She didn't like her hair. She watched her hide the gammon under the grapefruit rind. Rather peculiar hands. Ugly. Why did she keep looking out of the window? They heard Pete's car drive through the gates.

'I didn't say goodbye to him, Primrose.' The ram should be thanked. He'd been kinder in his way than Primrose.

'He's making some home calls.' For Peter's work didn't stop on Sunday. Solid as the Bank of England in his velvet-collared coat he went on tending his flock, keeping them solvent. Primrose had hastened his departure, not wanting him to see more of Ruth. She wanted her off the premises. She didn't seem to appreciate their home. Let her go back to the market. Refusing home-cooked food, ogling Pete, lolling in their best room like a tart. She hoped she had no kind of

30

infection. Had she been writing nasty things in that diary? She supposed she'd have to buy gifts for Ruth for years to come, offer her kindness. She looked slitty-eyed, queer enough for a breakdown. Her moneyspinner must be kept from her. She'd made sure he didn't see that hair flopping all over the lemon pillow case, or smell her scent again. She'd give away the nightdress. Mrs. Pluto would be glad of it. She'd make a note of it. Primrose wrote many notes, of reminder to herself, to 'Thoughtfully', to the men from 'Nicer Nooks' and Mrs. Pluto. Writing them gave her a divine pleasure, the only words she wrote. Peter had his secretary. Pens were necessary in Weybridge. She said she'd drive Ruth back, speed her away. She waited impatiently while she brushed her pointy teeth and combed her hair. She'd seen the milk down the bidet. Wasteful tart.

The leaves in the broad streets were swept into neat piles in the gutters. There was Sunday quiet. Primrose snuggled her fingers into the furred cover on her steering wheel, her mind dwelling on the pheasants in her oven. What pudding would Pete fancy? She rather regretted not having rung for a taxi for Ruth. Ruth was beyond redemption, beyond Miss Chips of Charm. She'd drop her near the market, get back to her pheasants.

Church bells were ringing, their tingling a reminder of the garden of her childhood. Sunday quiet, sun on cold leaves, bells ringing, were nostalgic. It was a relief to get out of Primrose's car, feeling her critical eyes for the last time. She'd put a box of Turkish Delight into Ruth's hands, a last minute sop to conscience. It was good to hear the bells. The garden lady used to say that a grateful heart was something to be cultivated. Children accepted moralising unquestioningly. A workman watched the car, watched her get out, straightening from piling the market refuse into a skip. He'd seen her, knew her, often shouted 'Morning, Red' at her. He wouldn't mind a bit like her, small, hot stuff probably, every man's dream. He liked the way her hair flapped when she ran. In no state for running now. The other one, the one with yellow hair, had no place in Notting Hill. Londoners varied. The yellow one, the one warm in her big car and furry clothes, would never see a rent book, nor would she travel underground, or put shillings in a gas meter. The redhead was a goer.

The wind blew frost-cold papers from tomato crates against her legs. The cold made her nose ache. She dumped the Turkish Delight in a litter-bin. An orange rolled as her foot touched it, to burst in a grey furred pulp by the kerb near the Emporium. It squished with a small sigh. Old fruit, vegetables, boxes and paper were everywhere. The bells rang on, at differing pitches and speed. A little girl stood with her back to Ruth, her hood concealing her face as she looked into the Emporium window. As Ruth drew level she turned, showing a flattened face, vacant, cruel, with eyes like the old doll's eyes. Like the doll she had a brown cloak. She made a growling in the back of her throat as she came towards Ruth.

'What do you want? Get back. Get away.'

Ruth tried to push her off, to get out of her reach. The child wouldn't stop, coming at her with hard red fists, hitting her, aiming at her stomach.

She smelled. Ruth felt her hard fists hitting. The hood fell back showing the thick neck, mis-shapen skull. She growled again. She had thin patchy hair.

'Stop. Get out of my way,' Ruth ran, her sandals slipping on the frosted cobbles. Her shawl tripped her. She heard the growling following her. She rang the bell, not waiting, ringing, ringing. Be in Logan, be in. The girl was after her. Be there.

She heard the stair-rail rattle. Then Logan was in the doorway looking down. She banged the door shut, stood shaking by the stair-rail.

Upstairs the kitchen was warm. The radio was on. The ice-plant tapped the window, the brown leaves had blown away to leave the stalks like withered bones. All the leaves from the plane trees were down.

4

'I'm so glad, Logan. So glad you were here.'

He said nothing, unwrapping her from her thick black shawl. You could judge character by the way people touched. It was difficult to think of him as Jordan's brother. Jordan was eldest, Logan the youngest of the family. They must have played once. Logan had left the lighted oven door open, adding to the fan-heater's warmth. The cold of Primrose's friendship, the cold of the weather, the cold of her fright, were gradually displaced. A late wasp crawled over the table. Logan picked it up by its wings, opening the window to put it on the stalks. She told him about the cloaked child.

'So that's why you rushed in. What was she like?'

Safe in the kitchen again, it seemed ridiculous. The child must have been playing. A nuisance only, of no more importance than the crawling wasp. Her likeness to the doll was coincidence. The doll under the divan was nothing more than a plaything left over from a long dead child. Dead children's toys were relics, not alarming. Logan told her not to be imaginative.

'But she did go for me. I didn't imagine that. Her eyes, her hands, were awful.' She fiddled with the buttons on her smock. She told about the noise the child had made, her thick-shaped head.

Logan went to the window again. No one there, only Mick the workman piling rubbish together, ready for disposal. Logan knew everybody in the market, the cleaners, dustmen, traffic wardens, as well as all the costermongers. He was their friend. The district drew itinerants, the newly-arrived. Jamaicans, Pakistanis came in increasing numbers. Old residents resented this. They grumbled. New flats were planned to replace the old unsafe buildings. Families came and went. Re-housing was a common topic. Logan said the child must be a recent arrival. The kitchen smelled of methylated from the cleaned windows. He said he'd make coffee. Unlike Jordan he liked the market as much as she did. It was colourful. Jordan had behaved indefensibly, but Logan had him to thank for his presence in Ruth's kitchen. Because of Jordan he was calming her, listening to her tell of some extraordinary little child. He said Ruth was too much alone. Obviously she hadn't benefited by her stay with Primrose. He stretched his hand out over the table. He said she looked unwell. He liked looking at her, had thought her beautiful on sight.

'You're not at all like Jordan, are you?'

'And you are not like anyone.' He wondered what she'd ever seen in Jordan who had always been self-absorbed. He had little belief in Jordan's work; he bragged too much. He wondered if Ruth liked making a martyr of herself for others. He'd liked to sketch the simple hugeness of her belly against the table. Her long-shaped eyes, her pellucid skin were arresting. And those bones. He'd never seen such pale-toned cheeks. He liked her way of dressing. He felt gratitude to Jordan.

'My stay with Primrose wasn't a success. Tell me about Dorset, Jordan never told me anything. What was it like, why did he hate it so?' She'd met no one but Logan, no relative had come to their Registry office wedding. Primrose sent a telegram.

'Jordan and I were once on good terms. At school. We went to the same school. The rest of the family are still at home, still in Dorset. All boys. I never want to go back either.'

'Why?'

'We weren't happy. There were six of us. My father was . . . is an Undertaker. The boys were automatically expected to work in the firm.'

He said that his mother died after he was born.

'An Undertaker? How awful, Logan. I had no idea.' Understandable that Jordan hated home, why he never mentioned it or his family of grave-diggers. Perhaps his reason for not wanting children came from that. An Undertaking father must have been worse, even more damnable than a museum porter.

'The firm has been in the family for generations. My father is semi-retired. The four boys run it now.' Jordan and he had not been able to take the work and all it entailed, and left for good.

'Tell me.'

He told how he hated profiting from distress. Jordan with his stomach had revolted first, had left for London. His father had shouted, had said his first-born should be disinherited. Logan followed in his path as soon as he was old enough, working at various jobs before he linked up with Jordan in Fyste Close, renting his garage for convenience. He couldn't take the work. The principle was wrong. Undertakers should be state-owned, no one getting rich. Funeral parlours thrived at the expense of grief. Two world wars and a recession brought increasing affluence to the firm of Cash & Whaler.

'Wasn't there anything? Anything you liked at all?'

'Having no mother didn't help. I grew up guilty. I don't remember much. I liked the countryside.' He spoke about the changing crops, oats, barley, wheat, the differing green fields that shaded purplish at twilight, the small wild flowers growing in the shelter of Purbeck stone walls. Of night owls, poppies and dog-roses. The insect collection shared with Jordan was a happy memory, though Jordan was cruel when it came to killing. Disgust of their father united them. His father used to shout. 'What is wrong with burying? That Grammar School has given you ideas.' Because of burying the two could stay at the better school. The other four left at fifteen. Disposal was an art. Morticians mattered.

They dignified a troubled scene, established order. They touched what other people wouldn't touch, they took what others wouldn't take. How dare Jordan and Logan carp about it, skive off after insects and pleasure. Life was serious. The firm of Cash & Whaler had earned much respect due to generations of hard work. Ingrates, why couldn't they be like the rest, help, support the firm to greater glory? First Jordan, then Logan, it was unjust.

'Yet you two weren't friends later?"

He said their old closeness was gone, forgotten; exchange of rent the only contact. Geographically close, they'd not regained comradeship.

'Did you ever get used to the funerals?'

'We were misfits. As I say, it runs in families.' Jordan and he wanted living work, not working with the dead. Logan wanted to depict life as he interpreted it, wanted to make constructions for touching, to be seen, not hidden under the earth. His art was for experiencing. His father's pride in his cosmetic work was sickening, the art of painting corpses to improve them. He felt sickened by the embalming, injecting fluid into the abdominal cavity and lungs. Organising hearses, walking in procession with a solemn face was a sickening way of making money. Thoughts of the patched cadavers in the coffins slipping from the lowering ropes onto the graves' foundations sickened him. He hated the crying and the black. All that his father loved and took pride in sickened him. For his father it was the stuff of life, the worse the world the better the burials. Since inflation the price of burials had rocketed. At school the boys had laughed. 'What Undertaker? I wouldn't care to live in your home. A living death.'

He and Jordan got teased about their names. When his mother died, at his birth, his father had been mother to the family. The smell of embalming fluid clinging to male clothing, earth, ashes, weeping and praying over coffin lids at low temperatures in their Chapel of Rest, was all too sickening. Logan loved the smell of Ruth, living and real.

She asked what they actually did to the stiffs. Not attractive, he told her. The plugging of nostrils, bandaging parts together, reassembling the results of mutilation to rough similitude, settling hair. Bodies donated to hospitals were returned after students had done what they wished, discovered disease, inside plastic bags. A corpse's brain quickly turned fluid. His father liked the prettying best, dusting with faint pink the loved ones, peaceful, lovelier after he'd finished with them than they'd been in life. His father never laughed.

'What happened when you left?'

'Like Jordan I left for good. He joined the library as you know. I worked on the railways for a time. Always interested in mechanics. Then I came here.' He used to hear Jordan at nights, at his kitchen table, slowly trying to write, or walking the floor to speed the muse. When Ruth moved in it changed his life. He watched for her going in and out. She fascinated him, he couldn't get her out of his thoughts.

'You have a girl, haven't you? Somebody you live with?'

'Leslie. I have Leslie.'

'But you will go on renting here, won't you? You'll stay?'

'Of course. I want to.'

'It was damnable of Jordan. I can't understand it.'

'I know. But don't be frightened.' Fear made you less able to contend. It was important to go on trying to trust.

She said it wasn't fear so much. Not knowing, not knowing where you stood was worse than fear. He understood her. Fear and not knowing were intrinsic to his childhood. Fear of his father's work, fear of what went on behind the mortuary doors, not knowing what the bodies looked like. Fear that he'd caused his mother's death, cost her her life's blood. Not knowing, fearful that he had caused a death that made his father's clothing smell. In Leslie he had found a new life style.

'Tell me about Leslie.'

'It's not the same as it used to be. When we first met. We're not happy recently.' Not since Ruth had come to the Close. He'd changed then. He asked her if he could do some sketches of her, sitting at the table.

'Of course.' Like old times, helping artists. She asked if she could get paper for him. He roughed in quickly, concentrating with thick frowning brows. His jersey elbow was darned neatly. Perhaps Leslie had darned it. Ruth wondered if Leslie was beautiful. There was Sunday peace in the kitchen.

She told him that she hated rows, told about her mother's shouting drunkenly at night, about her whines for money and her quiet father bearing it. How she'd resented him. Logan said a calamitous childhood needn't scar you, she needn't be a tragedy queen. You couldn't forget hurts, but you could build on them, turn them to advantage. He too had flashbacks that would always upset him, that he absorbed somehow.

'What kind?'

He shaded her belly with hard black strokes. One day he would tell about the corpse washed up at Chesil Beach, a bloated shapeless thing after time and salt water had done its work. They had to make a special coffin after the rushed inquest. The girl had drowned herself, was unrecognisable. After the funeral he'd had his first date. He'd never kissed anyone until that day. The smell of the battered body, the feel of it preyed on him. He'd kissed the girl in his arms and thought about the body. He touched her, touched her open lips, her open legs and thought about the body. She was immoderate. Her fat white limbs, her lips, her opened legs revolted him and he had almost vomited on her. Fat limbs still disgusted him. Part of the reason he wasn't enamoured of Primrose. He'd not kissed anyone again until he met Leslie in London. Leslie, thin, brown, wiry, had been an antidote until recently, when quarrelling had spoiled their ability to relate. The lid of the coffin had squished, closing on the suicide. He'd remembered the sound when he'd first seen Primrose getting from her car. He needed tenderness, to give and to receive love. He needed to be needed. Leslie was a grasper, a hard person. Ruth, by contrast was entirely feminine. She needed protecting. He liked small children, he looked forward to the arrival of a niece or nephew. He put his pencil down. Not half a bad sketch in a short time.

'Logan, I wonder if you could advise me.' Not shy with him she leaned her elbows on the table. She'd not liked asking at the Clinic in case they scoffed, in case the condition was a standard one. Her nipples kept shrivelling, exuding drops of liquid, was it natural did he think?

Logan said no doubt it was the body preparing, getting ready for the birth. He had enjoyed biology, the study of change, mutation, birth. He looked with interest at her breast through the unbuttoned smock. Her bluish veins were pretty, like veining on the wings of a cabbage white. Her pointed breasts were delicate. Did she intend breast feeding?

'I hate the thought. I'm sore already without a baby biting at me, damn it.'

'They don't bite, Ruth.'

'It looks as if they do.' She felt relaxed, protected by his hand touching her. He talked about the birth. Growth was a miracle. He'd like to model her in clay, cast it in iron. What did she think? An abstract work, like all his work, based on her seated figure. He might call it 'Fruition'. It would be a shared enterprise. She nodded, stimulated by the thought of working with artists again, artists looking at her, envisaging their future work and talking. Back in the harness, helping art. Logan didn't brag. She liked the title. What names did he like for her baby?

'Merlin?' A name of strength, of permanence and legend.

'A wizard, wasn't he? I don't much like that one. What about Maris for a girl?'

He told her it meant belonging to the sea. He didn't like reminders of sea water. Too much of the past in it. The sea was cruel, claiming its yearly quota of bodies, washed up with seaweed in their hair. Ruth was as soft-haired as a mermaid. She had a singing quality in her voice. He listened while she told him of her love of words. Sometimes she invented them. He understood. Being caressed by him made her forget Weybridge, forget about the market child.

"I tricked Jordan into marrying me,' she said. Marriage didn't ensure security.

He understood that too. He asked if she had everything ready.

'What ready?'

'Ready for the birth. It's due soon. You should have everything.'

'I'm not ready at all. I've nothing.' No cot, no woolly things and shawls. She felt ashamed. Because Jordan had taken the case she'd put the lists of clothing out of her mind.

His feather-stitched brows looked stern. She should have more forethought. She was responsible for a life. Because Jordan was feckless was no reason for her to be. Clothes, a cot, would not appear by themselves. It was unfair not to provide for a child she'd started purposely. She had an obligation.

'Oh Logan.'

He touched her again, unable to resist it before buttoning her smock. He longed to start 'Fruition'. Her eyes, her jawbone sloped with such interesting contrast against the fall of her shoulders and her stomach. She had quite ugly hands. You always found a flaw highlighting beauty. He used to think about becoming an artist years ago when sickened by the rotten bodies and the smell of Interflora vans. New wood, modelling clay, cast iron were the smells he wanted round him. And Ruth. Had she got her lists?

She fetched them from the bedroom. He needed her. Modelling made you feel necessary. She'd started in the first place to punish her father for saddling her with such a mother, to upset and shock him. Then she'd enjoyed it. You didn't feel alone when you posed, part of a creative act, included in the venture. Both their fathers were responsible for their desire to record, to leave something behind. She'd never read 'For Ruth, who made it all come true' on any book by Jordan. She would inspire 'Fruition'. Logan was truly committed to his work. Jordan had wanted her to keep a record of all he said and did, for future biographies about him, had objected to her diaries. A diary was self-orientated, took her thoughts away from him. Logan holding the list was concerned about provision for her child. She'd deserved reprimand. Both their fathers had been damnable in different ways.

'Look, it's starting to snow.'

Thick blobs were beginning to settle on the ice-plant stalks. The Sunday church ringing was muffled. They watched the flakes blurring the sky over the grey roof slates, settling over the weeds in the guttering opposite, filling the holes in the brickwork. He said they were in for a heavy fall.

'There's a rat there,' she said, grabbing his hand.

It ran across the Close, a blimp-shaped outline against the whitening cobbles. He looked put out. He had suspected it. He'd got rid of her mice for her. Rats were more serious. They liked the market; bad weather made them restless, they ran for warmer quarters, for food more edible than refuse frozen in the gutters. She said he mustn't trap them, trapping was cruel. It didn't matter if they stayed outside, what did one rat matter? He said where there was one you got more.

'It doesn't matter if they do no harm.' It was humans who made havoc, of their own and others' lives. She hadn't minded mice running round her cooker, though with a baby they were better gone. He'd used small traps with bread.

She took her shawl from the wall.

'You're not going out again? In the snow? I've bought food, what do you want?'

She said she was going to the Emporium to see her friend Podesta Doge.

'Why, Ruth? Don't.' He wanted to show her his fruit machine, a fairground relic made to take old halfpennies. His plan now was to incorporate it in 'Fruition'. Ruth said she had missed her Saturday talk with the Doge. She would be worrying about her. She'd see his fruit machine on her way out. He helped her down the stairway. That stair rail wasn't safe. He'd bought unusual cheeses for her, granary bread and mixed nuts to tempt her appetite. The flat would be as good as human hands could make it before the arrival of his niece or nephew.

At the back of the garage his real work, his art, was done. He'd put a window in the end wall for the north light. Once all the flats over the garages had been lived in, before the process of ruination started. Now only No. 3 was lived in, kept neat, with window-boxes. Each had its garden, wildernesses, separated by rotting fencework. Logan's new window showed a lawn with weeds growing to the height of the withered currant bushes round it. Outside the window were pieces of larger sculpture, strange cast-iron shapes. He intended to make the lawn habitable before the summer. There were two pear trees at the end. With the whirling snow it looked like the paperweights you shook to make the flakes tumble, a magic place. He wanted to build steps down from her bathroom window, to save coming through the garage to get there. At the far end of the garden the wall was cracked in a zigzag split, though snow was already giving it a balanced neatness, filling the masonry. The pear tree branches bent whitened arms over the currant bushes. By the summer time she wouldn't recognise it, he told her, a perfect shelter for a child's pram. Inside the garage the fruit machine dominated everything. He pinned the sketch he'd done upstairs near it. He thought about his sculpture while he did his repairing by day, starting his real work at night. He liked incorporating random objects, admired Man Ray, Duchamp, who'd made use of differing textures. Ruth wondered if Leslie minded him out late. The fruit machine was solid, old. The garage was cold.

Over the door of the Emporium the Doge had painted 'Lady Podesta Doge' in copper plate. Her paintwork was dark red, now looking almost black against the snowy market. The objects in her window were jumbled interestingly in front of a huge distorting mirror from a tunnel of fun, separating the window display from the shop interior. The people liked the mirror, on warm bright days it didn't distort much, at night or when the light was grey it could make you look horrendous. The little market child had looked in it when Ruth came home earlier. Flat irons, boot scrapers, bellows, butter churns, old sieves could all be bought at Lady Podesta Doge. Her other speciality was oils from the orient. She made these herself from secret ingredients. Ruth looked at herself. She looked like a young mad monk. The Doge heard her step on the painted stairway.

'My one, my one, I'm up here cooking. I'm cooking something special. I knew you'd come today. Puss knew too.'

41

The smell from the Doge's cooking was like a blow on the nostrils, a stench that nearly made you retch. She loved experimenting. Anything edible, the odder the better, went into her food. She'd got best rump steak from the butcher for her mince, into which she stirred sandal oil, cocoa, a little mashed sardine and a green concoction in a tin under the table she'd forgotten about. The Doge believed in accepting the hand of fate, and various spirits guided her from the other side. She hummed as she stirred. Ruth had liked that old dolly, she had something more, some oil of myrrh for her. 'Myrrh is mine, its bitter perfume, breathes a life of gathering gloom, sorrowing, sighing, bleeding, dying, sealed in a stone cold tomb.' The Doge had a raucous singing voice. If the snow kept up it would be lovely. Ruth's baby and a white Christmas. Rule Britannia.

Ruth sniffed the oil. Bitter, and a little sweet. 'The thing of it is, Doge, isn't it a bit sad?'

'No no, not sad. Not sad at all. Seasonable. I took a fancy to it.'

The Doge tapped her wooden spoon against her pot rim. She'd discovered long ago that the spirits of the cosmos liked smells. They lingered where smells were, smells fascinated them. For this reason her cooking was unusually strong, especially when combined with her oils. Her puss was not house-trained. Her particular spirit, her favourite guide, was a Genoese chief magistrate who seemed fond of sandal wood and mashed sardine, sending her special messages. Dabbling in occultism, reading hands and teacups as well as selling old things, enabled the Doge to save a little. She loved her oils. She claimed to do tarot readings, but didn't encourage clients, it was so complicated, her eyes weren't what they once were and it was a complicated task. She preferred listening with attention to what her people said, that way you learned a lot. She opened seven days a week. Unsnobbish, friendly, she was respected in the market. She liked Logan, a straight man to deal with. She'd had no truck with Jordan, though it didn't pay to judge others. She was extremely fond of Ruth. The Doge and Puss looked forward to her Saturday visits. She offered a dip of orange mince from the end of the spoon. The mince was burning. Ruth winced as she tasted. She looked at the Doge's loose grey bun, the tendrils falling into loops, looked at the oily pores round her nose, each pitted with a blackhead. The Doge had the greasiest skin, was one of the kindest people in the market. Ruth felt blessed. She had Logan and the Doge. The mince had the reek of a train lavatory.

'My one, you're troubled. I can sense it.'

Ruth told her about Weybridge. About Pete's crawly hands, about Primrose, the milk and bacon, the general suffocation of the place. She said Primrose had changed since moving. She told her about the child in the market, how she'd looked like the Doge's doll.

The Doge stood still over her pot. Drops of orange mince plopped from her spoon. She sneezed. 'My one, this could be quite important.'

'Er . . . where is the dolly please?' The spirits liked old things too.

'Its head came off. I cut its buttons off.' Ruth looked down at the pretty buttons showing through her shawl.

'Toys, a broken thing, is what a spirit likes.' They went for stressful situations. It might have been a sighting, the child might be the spirit who had the doll once. Near birth, near Christmas, conditions were capital.

'I don't believe all that, Doge. The child was mad, that's why she went for me.'

The Doge stirred quickly again. The mince was sticking, burning. Her wooden spoon tip was quite black. Nothing was coincidence, she said. The doll, buttons, old things, smells. What did the girlie look like?

Ruth said she was yellow-complexioned, mongoloid. Her hair was jet, thin in patches when her hood fell back.

'Believe, believe my one. You're Pisces aren't you?'

'Believe what? You know I'm Pisces, you did my horoscope.'

'Of course. Of course.' Pisceans were so curious, the most difficult of all. Pondering over those detailed charts made the Doge drowsy. She resorted to magazines, mixing forecasts with delicacy, a line here, a sentence there, usually pleased clients.

'Who could she have been, I wonder?'

'Er . . . come to my meeting. Eight o'clock. You know, my usual Wednesday meeting. Most probably it was an unquiet one, someone in spirit trying to get through.' Someone had a titbit of information for her Ruth. Pisceans were subject to divine inspiration, though much depended on the moon's positioning. Might there be epilepsy in the family? Ruth had had a loathsome mother certainly.

Her Wednesday seances were rarely well attended. She held them in her kitchen among the smells. Frequently no one came at all.

'I'm not a believer, Doge, you know that. I don't believe messages, titbits. My mother was a Catholic.' When brandy-filled her mother used to wail about lost souls, retribution, between requests for cash. Her patient father never answered back.

'A Roman Catholic? Really? Never mind.' The Doge wasn't keen on Romans, whose dogma forbade them consulting her. She had no quarrel with Christ, a true spiritualist, walking the waters, battling devils. Catholics were her worst customers. She'd like a word with that runaway mother, get Ruth's time of birth and ascertain about epilepsy. The Doge's life in the market was a come-down after her past one with her Genoese, when she'd had power and influence. Now she had to beg audiences, earn extra by selling tat. Every Wednesday she sat in her circle of dark red painted chairs, settling her bun and hoping. She had respect locally, that counted for a lot. Her knicknacks were good value, interestingly reflected in her mirror. She read a palm or two and didn't charge a lot. She was so fond of Ruth.

Ruth sniffed her myrrh-dabbed wrist-bones. Dabbling in mysticism was of no interest, what she already knew was enough. She wanted to put the market child out of her mind. The smell of the kitchen made her feel slightly giddy. She thanked the Doge for her present and left her looking sadly into her pot of blackened orange mince. Later she'd bottle some more oils, a cheering pastime, one of her favourites. She did it all, filling small phials from containers via a funnel. Her oils were collected from eastern barks, bought from the Indian, another market dignitary. She mixed and invented, labelling her bottles, 'Oil of Lost Spirits', 'Plaint', 'Tomb Essence'. She wore plastic rings that caught in the light of the brown and yellow oils.

'Er . . . don't forget now. I'll do you a reading any time' the Doge called down the stairs. Ruth's reflection in the darkening afternoon was more curious, madder. She laughed at the Doge behind her back, didn't take her seriously; her readings didn't tally. The love-lorn and the lonely would believe anything, particularly a denial of what they dreaded. She'd make her life take wing, get back to Logan and the Sunday peace. Logan was stalwart. She felt lucky, lucky to be hurrying back with a phial of oil, lucky to be breathing lungfuls of snow-cold air, lucky to have Logan as well as the Doge, whose kitchen turned her stomach. She would be confident, make the most of each moment, go with her luck, enjoy things. Soon she'd be lying in a hospital bed, being fed with trays of food, visited by two real friends, Doge and Logan.

Her kitchen in Number 3 smelled of coffee. Logan said the oil was strange, but it suited her.

5

'LOGAN, will you come? Logan?'

Since the small hours she'd waited for the sound of his garage doors scraping over the hard, packed snow as he opened them. Since the day they'd seen the rat fresh snow had fallen every night. Since the dawn light she'd waited in the silence. The world felt dead. Birds, the gradual stirring in the market, distant buses, vans, Mick the street-cleaner hailing a milkman, then the sound of Logan's doors. He shovelled the snow each morning. She shivered and worried, lying squeezed into a lump. She had no clock. She couldn't make herself get up and switch the fire on. Her breath steamed. There was ice inside the bedroom window. Now it would happen. Pain, wailing, pain and blood, pain, fright. There would be enemas, shaving, official forms and temperatures, more pain, the frightful pain that paved the path to deliverance. Rich or poor, you had the same anguish.

'It's happening, Logan.'

Everything was ready. The soft-topped case, bought specially with Jordan's cheque, had been most carefully packed. She'd fingered every item like an initiate. Logan had given her enthusiasm. The baby was well provided, vests, napkins, all-in-one sleeping suits with feet attached, designed to stretch as the child grew, that she'd chosen in dark colours. Her child would be unusual. She'd bought embroidered tunics for herself, to wear in bed. Her spongebag, aromatic soap and flannel matched. She hadn't ticked the dressing-gown, she'd borrow Logan's sweater, darned at the elbow, reaching to her knees. He'd given her a surprise, an electric toothbrush, guaranteed not to flick paste round the face. She planned to plug it over the hospital bed after her bloody anguish. She'd think about her child's future while polishing the spaces between her teeth.

'Hurry, Logan.'

'Don't panic, Ruth.' He forced his voice to calmness. She mustn't see that he was tired. Tired from a night of rowing with Leslie in

Ladbroke Grove. Their affair was over. Leslie was leaving. Drained dry, exhausted, Ruth mustn't know, not yet. He told her to lie still. He put his hand on her. You had to note the time as muscles tightened in contraction. He stroked her hands. Not yet, not yet.

'Brush your hair properly after you are up. And use the toothbrush. Did you try it yet?' She mustn't see how sad he felt. Relieved as well, to be rid of a love that had become a burden. He plugged the brush under the calendar of monarchs. Henry, the ring round his leather shoe, looked reproving. He stood watching Ruth, standing in the light from the snow-laden garden. Her long, worried eyes looked into his as she brushed up and down her molars. It made a soothing buzz. Plenty of time, he said, a first child never hurried. He switched it to low speed, told her to carry on, it would relax and freshen her. The light made their reflection greenish in the mirror. He told her to put on her buskin sandals, the red ones that he liked.

'I can't. I can't bend to fix them.'

'I'll do it. Sit. Let me.' He lead her to the kitchen. He loved her foot that almost fitted in his hand, the rings she wore, though her toes could have been cleaner. He crossed the thin red straps round her ankle. The length of her thin legs was what he'd first noticed when he'd seen her walk over Fyste Close cobbles, the stilted way she walked, like some strange water-paddling bird, all slung with leather ornaments. He wound the straps lovingly. He saw the water before she did. The trickle that turned into a gush, the gush a waterfall, falling onto his hands and round her red straps, running down the chair-leg in a stream.

'Good Christ, Logan. Look. The floor is flooded. It's coming out of me. Christ.'

'It's all right. Don't panic.'

'But it's coming out of me. What is it?'

He said it was her waters. The waters broke early sometimes, the amniotic fluid that enclosed the foetus. He spoke directively. She wasn't to worry. She was to stop whimpering. She was to sit on a towel. It simply meant they'd have to leave at once, not delay for a cup of coffee as he'd planned. His Rolls was finished, wasn't it lucky? A purple Rolls to convey her in comfort, re-sprayed, restored, ready. It wasn't far. He wiped her down. A good omen, she'd have a speedy birth. She needn't be frightened.

Her situation, taking charge of her, helped him to forget his night with Leslie, the termination of their affair. Life had a pattern, you learned to adjust, like floating with the tide. Ruth must not agitate. No need to speak of Leslie yet, just as there was no need yet to speak of Jordan's bounced cheque. He'd gone to the bank for Ruth. The cashier had looked grave, retired to the back to confer, returned to the counter still more lugubrious. Logan hadn't been surprised. He'd never put much trust in Jordan's honesty, or his writing, not since they shared a collection of insects. The cashier said that Jordan was overdrawn, there was no question of honouring his cheque. Where was he? Did he know? He'd told the cashier he'd no notion of his brother's whereabouts, was not his keeper. Jordan was a law to himself, it wasn't his affair. He left the bank, having drawn the money for Ruth from his own account. Then, from curiosity, he'd gone to Jordan's library. Was he all right? He wanted to hear news of his elder brother. The Chief Librarian looked at him, flat distaste in his pale eyes. Mention of Jordan Cash was an abomination. Jordan had left his branch, left without notice, had not been seen. No formal resignation, no speech over the teacups, no farewell gift in recognition of services rendered. Gone. Letters sent to an address in Kilburn had been returned marked 'Whereabouts unknown.' J. Cash had been a bounder. Earlier he had sympathised. Jordan had come to him. Wife-trouble, changing home, bad business. He'd given him the charge of a small branch library, a change and rest. He'd made an error. What transpired proved it. One morning Jordan failed to turn up. Punctuality, efficiency, attention to detail were essential in librarianship. Jordan had failed him. Outrages had come to light after his disappearance. He had not been painstaking. Records of overdue books were chaotic. Books were stolen, blacklisted borrowers allowed to re-join. A whole delivery of new books vanished without trace, before processing. Stationery had disappeared in quantity. There were verses scribbled over flyleaves, walls. Bounder. The Borough Council rarely made a mistake over character. To top it, the night before he vanished he'd had some kind of fit, had scattered tickets recording the loan of books, a system called Brown's Issue over the library floor, before vomiting into the empty trays. They'd had to close the premises. It took three library persons to remedy the damage. Ratepayers had complained. They weren't straight yet, his successor still chanced on trouble. Mention of his name in the staff room had been forbidden from that day. Logan explained again that he wasn't his brother's keeper. Most regrettable. Now, driving Ruth to hospital, he was responsible. Her waters wetting his hands involved him like a sacrificial rite. She needed him, had turned to him. He'd got there just in time.

She said her stomach didn't feel as tight now. He settled her comfortably in the Rolls. Before she left the kitchen she'd looked back. It would never be the same. Like a toll gate, or moving through a turnstile, she was moving into a different territory.

Her life would never be the same. The kitchen would wait while she was in hospital, while birth took place. The rosemary, the rue in the wall-rack, the dried bulrushes, cow parsley in the jar, would wait. The fittings, divan, table would no longer be just hers, her child would share them. This would be her child's home. She'd give the child unconditional love. She felt immensely isolated.

The air outside hurt when you spoke. It hurt your nose and ears. Logan had put the toothbrush on top of her things, before snapping the soft-topped case shut. He hadn't swept the snow. Their feet creaked over it. Snow had settled in the plane tree, thickening angles between the twigs and branches, padding the window sills of the Close. No ice plant stalks showed. Birds left clawmarks. Snow had a barely discernible smell, a sharpness in the mouth. At the entry of the Close wheels had made criss-cross tracks. Logan buckled her seatbelt, not tired now, thinking only about her.

'Look Logan. Another. Over there.' She held his wrist. Together they looked at the rat in front of the garage. Its flat-eared face looked back at the purple car. He saw the larger tracks made by its feet. He'd shut the doors. Its face was desperate.

He said that did it. He'd put down poison. The old buildings were a health hazard. It was unsafe.

Ruth said she'd rather have a cat, though she didn't like them. The Doge's Puss, supposed to help, to encourage psychic happenings and act as a familiar, did nothing but smell and dribble. 'There's another pain'. She bent over the seat-strap with clenching teeth. He said remember to breathe quietly, to stay calm. The Rolls was running like a bird, thanks to his work. Her maiden trip, running Ruth to hospital to be delivered, was a proud mission. Breathe slowly, don't think about rats or cats, at her age birth was nothing. She'd sail through if she stayed calm. As if to confirm his words a weak sun shaft shone. A little snow fell from the plane tree over them, glittering on the dark bonnet of the Rolls. Ruth sat on a rolled towel in case of further dribbles. Her red straps still felt wet. They passed the Emporium. A placard stuck in her mirror read 'Consult Podesta Doge this Christmas. Learn something to your advantage. Spiritual messages Wednesday eight o'clock.'

Though everything Ruth had expected took place, she liked it. She liked the students bending over her, gravely discussing her slender build. Dry first births weren't usual. She liked the silvery trumpets that the nurses held, pressing them and listening to her. She liked them taking notes. She liked their various hands, pale, freckled or dark-skinned, pressing her. She liked the Sister with the fluted cap curled round like little horns, who changed to meekness when the doctor came.

'Well done, mother, you're at the final stage.' If only every patient were as compliant, as eager to help themselves as Mrs. Cash. 'Push now dear, pant like an animal. Push, push.'

The Sisters' and the nurses' bleating was echoed by a smaller weaker sound coming from inside. 'Push, push, there now.'

Out slid something sticky, something like Turkish Delight, a bleating sticky redness, warm between her thighs. 'The easiest birth you ever knew, there now.' A natural, they said, the child had come out crying. No need to smack, just wipe her mouth out, swab round, wrap her, there now, give her to her mother. Wrapped clean, now wasn't that a joy. A joyful birth and not a second's woe. A Wednesday's child was supposed to be woeful. Born in record time and not a bleep out of the mother.

'Are her hands all right?'

'Her hands? Why shouldn't they be? Why hands?'

'Is she all right?'

'Of course she is. Give her a chance, she's not five minutes old. She's perfect.' Newborns were like moths, all crumpled from the chrysalis, damp, wrinkled still. Hands indeed. Give her a chance. She was a lucky mother, a lovely infant, hubby with a purple car who'd stayed with her till near the end. What more could you ask?

Ruth looked into the small face. She looked a bit like Logan. She'd heard that the face you thought of during intercourse resulted in a

50

like-faced child. The time she'd thrown away her cap she remembered wondering about Logan. Lying under Jordan in the mornings, she listened to the garage doors opening, wondered about Logan and his art. Two brothers, writer, sculptor, two so different. Jordan was never tender. Logan said her diary-keeping was important, encouraged her. Now she had something else to show him, the baby in her arms, looking like her uncle, smelling of Turkish Delight.

'What name will you call her? Have you thought, mother?'

Ruth looked again. Her hair was an orange shadow on her pate. She had a neat-shaped skull, flat ears, red lashes just discernable under neat-sketched brows. They wheeled her, still holding the baby, into the post-natal ward.

'Tangerine. Her name is Tangerine.'

'A Tangerine? That's rare. That's very rare. Flower names, yes, fruit never. Did you hear Sister? We never had a Tangerine.'

Ruth kissed the orange head. It sounded right. She looked at her all over. She opened her curled hands. Her palm looked waterlogged, the slivered nails cutting the flesh. She had an adult face as though she should have teeth. She pulled her top lip to make sure. Sleeping now, having lain nine months in a bag of water that had burst over the kitchen floor and Logan. She was miraculous, might marry royalty or be a ballerina. The Doge would predict a starry future. She'd be the loveliest thing in the market.

Everybody chattered. It was over. You complained about the terror of the delivery room, the after pains which could be as nasty as labour ones almost. The food was rotten, the nurses worse. You let off steam, made friends with those in neighbouring beds. Ruth stayed quiet. Bathing in light must feel like this; Tangerine's hair was so soft.

Nurse Asuni took Tangerine from her. She must rest, the child must get used to the cradle.

'Come through then? All right are you? There's nothing I don't know about birthing. Watch that nig-nog nurse. Steal the skin off your teeth, she would.'

Ruth's neighbour, Mrs. Copper, was chummy. Inquisitive too. She'd never seen a mother without some kind of dressing-gown. An old darned sweater wasn't quite the thing for hospital. Nothing else was shabby about her, she'd never seen such nighties, black as an Arab, the red part clashing with her hair. A freaky girl, artist or somesuch she wouldn't mind betting. She'd never seen a mother who lay twiddling her hands instead of preparing herself for visiting like everybody else. Powder from compacts clouded the air, lipsticks were rubbed over lips that temporarily stopped complaining. Once they were made up the patients didn't grouse as loudly, keeping their eyes on the door for their loved ones. Mrs. Copper never had a visitor, though she lipsticked just the same. She came in every year. She'd quickly spotted Ruth's electric toothbrush. She longed to use it on her few loose teeth. She'd heard it toned the gums. With good teeth you kept a grip on life. She asked if Ruth's husband was coming.

'Old Copper is a layabout. Bricklayer by trade, layabout by nature. He never comes. Not that birthing is anything special. One tiddler is much like another. I'm past caring. You first-timers all think you've won the jack-pot. Wait until your first half-dozen. Not that red hair isn't pretty. I thought first that you'd dyed yours. Then I saw your tiddler's.' For the next hour she would hold her paper up, to show she didn't care that no one came to her bedside. She listened, speculated as to the income, background, social standing of each visitor, shielded by her paper. For all that Arab get-up Ruth seemed a nice sort.

Logan touched her hair. He touched Tangerine, cupping her round head in the cradle. He lifted her, supporting her head in the crook of his elbow. She had a mouth like Ruth's. She was Ruth's miniature.

'That's right, support the head, don't rock her. Rocking ruins them.' Mrs. Copper poked her head from round her paper. She approved of Logan, a man who understood a tiddler's needs and owned a flash saloon. She wouldn't mind a ride. Dare she ask for a loan of that toothbrush?

'I liked it, Logan. I liked the whole thing. At the ending I had to pant like a dog. She felt like a lump of Turkish Delight coming out. She smells nice, doesn't she?'

Mrs. Copper put down the paper. Visitors like this were worth birthing for, worth loneliness. She mustn't miss a word. It was her lucky day. 'My own are winners too,' she called. She could line them up like steps of a stair. Now she was grateful to Logan for taking an interest in her newst one, tidy in its cradle. Old Copper never looked at them till they were big enough to kick. Yes, she was an authority on birthing. Pity the nig nurse spoiled things, her and her light fingers.

52

Ruth was freaky all right, sniffing her tiddler, calling it an orange. Her Logan wasn't complaining of anything, you'd think he'd won the Pools.

He'd brought a pot of Christmas berries, shining among dark leaves. Mrs. Copper said better not let the nig nurse catch sight of them, nigs liked a bit of colour. The berries made a pretty show, just like his daughter's hair. She was past caring about flowers. She had no gifts on her locker, nothing but a pile of papers. She watched Ruth and Logan hanging worshipfully over Tangerine. She told them those curved mauve spindly legs were natural. Ruth thought they were like claws. Mrs. Copper suggested Holly was more of a seasonal name. Was Ruth religious?

'I may have been baptised Catholic. I'm not sure.' Ruth smelled her child again. She smelled holy. Her only obligation was to be a worthwhile mother. Mrs. Copper sent her tiddlers to the Mission for the sake of peace once a week. What was Logan?

He said he was agnostic. He sometimes wished he had a faith, but his reason outruled it. There was his work. His salvation was in his search for truth in sculpture.

'What do you do then, Logan? Not that I'm nosy, just curious.'

'I have my workshop. General repairing.' He didn't talk about his sculpture. It was Ruth who explained to Mrs. Copper about his constructions, the work he did after hours. Sculpture was his real work.

'Sculpture? I love sculpture.' Where would London be without Nelson and all them stone generals. Ruth was a lucky Arab. Somebody to show art to her, to drive her round and give her electrical contraptions.

'She's going to wake up, Logan. Look.' But Tangerine only stirred deeper into sleep. Mrs. Copper raised her paper again. A ward could be a lonely place without visitors.

'Ruth, shall I get in touch with your mother?'

'My mother? Why? She's nothing to me. Why?'

'She's Tangerine's grandmother. She ought to be told.' A child should have caring relatives. Ruth's mother had a right to know, to give or withhold her love. He still had nightmares about his mother, of her bleeding, dying in order to give him birth. Ruth's mother ought to be told, given the chance to decide.

'She shouldn't, damn it. I want nothing from her. Ever.' Her mother

53

stayed away eleven years. Why trace her?

'Go on, Logan. Tell. I agree.' Mrs. Copper poked out from her paper, unable to resist. He had the right idea. Tell, put the granny in the picture.

'How she responds is up to her. But give her the chance. Where might she be?'

'I've no idea. Nor do I care. She left when I was nine. She went.' She'd come in from school, not long after her mother fetched her from the garden lady. Home in Battersea was no different, her mother was worse, popped pills into her mouth as well as brandy. The same mess in each room, same smell. Her mother was disastrous. Why tell?

'I only wish I had one.' Somebody to care about her instead of only Old Copper. Where would the world be without mothers? She folded her paper, leaned across the space between the beds. Ruth hadn't had it rosy, that was plain. Her mother hadn't been quite the thing, had scarpered, left the little Arab. Perhaps she'd loved her Dad, before he passed away?

'My father brought me up, after my mother left. Before that, I was fostered for some while.' Ruth bent over Tangerine's fingers, uncurling them, seeing her father's face again, dull, kind, worried. In death he had looked just as worried, white against the satin of the coffin. No cosmetic work for him; the plainest box. Where was he? Would he like his grandchild? Would he be prouder of Tangerine than he'd been of her? Lowering herself, not realising her capabilities, he'd been ashamed of Ruth's carry-ons. A pity he had died instead of her damnable mother. Would Cash & Whaler have charged less than she'd paid for his cremation?

Mrs. Copper reckoned Ruth was lucky though. A sculpture business downstairs, a granny somewhere, Logan. Mrs. Copper was sick of doing everything. Old Copper was a liability, had never bought a toothbrush in his life.

'Look, Logan. Look, the Doge.' Ruth raised herself, her yellow eyes alert. The Doge had come to pay homage.

All the patients had noticed Ruth, her colouring caused stares, plus her clothes. The Doge attracted a different kind of notice, a sight you didn't reckon on, especially in hospital. She glided in with short quick steps, her feet and thin calves hidden by her cloak. She always hid her calves under long clothing. She smiled to right and left, ensuring her rightful notice. She'd put pink powder over her blackheads, patchily. Each finger flashed with plastic. Her cloak hung in stiff folds. She'd stitched signs of the zodiac in gaudy felts round the hem. The mothers were reminded of church, of weddings, baptisms and death. She made you think of serious things, made you remember that in the midst of birth there was another side. With birth came death and all that guff. Excitedly, a bit uneasily, they watched the Doge go up to Ruth, a grin on her face. She'd gone to pains. Some of her spirits were shy. Bright colouring as well as smells encouraged them. She'd stitched motifs around her button holes.

'My one, your time is over. Er . . . dear little Gingernut.' She gestured towards the bundle Logan held. She sneezed before pressing Ruth to her embroidered bosom. She had little interest in babies.

'Oh Doge.'

'The mystic influence will never desert you. Believe, believe. And how is bo-in-law?' Poor fellow, he looked exhausted. He worked too hard. How kind to involve himself in the brat's birth.

'Sit down here, Doge.' Logan offered his chair. He put the baby in her cot, sat close to Ruth, his arm along her pillow. The only sign that she'd been through an ordeal was her smell, her hair smelled rank, a smell rather like a cat. Excitement heightened the senses, alerted his visionary eye, his third eye he called it. His brain signalled. It had all happened. The group round the bed, the smell, the faces of the Ward, shapes, colours, were an echo from another time. Like a religious group Ruth and her child were the heart. The people stared with bovine eyes. The Doge had brought gifts.

Mrs. Copper's attention was riveted. What, brother-in-law, not husband? Was Logan Tangerine's uncle? Uncles, grannies, this queer church lady, it was as good as a cartoon. She watched the Doge take packets from her cloak. A gilded fish on a thong, to hang up or to wear, some strangely scented oil, unusual cigarettes.

'I never smoke, Doge. But thank you all the same. The fish is attractive. Thank you.'

'These puffs won't hurt, my one. These puffs are beneficial. Look, made from the young leaves of gooseberry bushes. Daily inhalation by the young and not so young. Effective in all bodily and mental ills. Banish illness by smoking gooseberry leaves.'

Logan said he'd like to try, but he'd given up too, even his pipe. The fish was a mystic sign used by early Christians, did Doge know that? The Doge gave him a pitying look. It was astrological, Ruth's birth-sign.

'I'm Virgo myself,' said Mrs. Copper, wishing she was a virgin. She took a cigarette, trying not to snatch. At last. She was included.

The Doge raised her jewelled fingers. She felt magisterial. From that moment she decided she'd cast no more horoscopes. The strain of it was too great, in case the same person came again. She'd stick to meetings and spiritual palmistry. Luckily she knew everyone's business in the market. She had contacts. Mick the street-cleaner picked up information along with rubbish, would tell for a small sum. There was a Mr. Bent who sold fruit very cheaply. He had financial dealings in other ways with the market populace, he knew secrets. There was the Indian. The smoke rose strong and grey about the two beds. Mrs. Copper asked to see the packet. The information sounded queer.

'Er . . . a translation from Sanskrit.' The Indian did the Doge's printing. The smoke annoyed Nurse Asuni. That smell was unhygienic. Was the old lady taking drugs? It was annoying for the other patients. Such thick smoke obscured their view, especially for the ones like Mrs. Copper who had no one. Was she annoying them purposely? Unconcerned, the Doge peered back, narrowing her stubby top and lower lashes. She always kept a lookout for possible clients.

'Lady, are you Ruth's Aunty? Care for a read of the paper?' Mrs. Copper thrust her *Daily Mirror* out.

'No Ta. Not her Aunt. A very dear friend. I've known Logan too for years.'

Mrs. Copper said pay no attention to the nig nurse. Devil. Lowering the tone. They never should be let into the country.

The Doge didn't answer. She bowed her head over her cigarette, drawing deeply. Life had taught her when to stay silent, when to speak. Relationships, a person's colour or physique, were pre-ordained. You must accept. There were the ruled and ruling. Her bread and butter depended on frailty. Nig, white, handicapped, what matter? What mattered was a person's problems. Without problems clients wouldn't need her. She guessed that Mrs. Copper's life was burdensome. When lives became unbearable they came to her. Paid cash to be told that what they feared wouldn't happen. They couldn't understand it, life wasn't fair, what had they done to be punished? The Doge knew that love lit in the oddest places, uniting hearts unsuitably. An illness, death, protracted litigation, a broken heart, were profitable to the Doge. Heartbreak mattered. Not that she willed, she had the greatest sympathy, offered a helping hand. She hated newspapers.

Ruth explained that the Doge told fortunes. Mrs. Copper stretched her hand out. She'd like to be told that this new tiddler was her last.

'My Emporium, the Market,' the Doge said sharply. She never worked for nothing, except for Ruth. She would bargain rather than refuse a client outright. Throughout her life she'd heard the strangest wails, as, bent over cups or palms, she wondered what to tell them. They wailed of love and money, love and indifference, love and the stamina to keep the loved one loving. Money usually came into it. The fear of failing to achieve a happy state. They wailed of dreadful happenings and woe. Sometimes she felt like saying, 'Fail then, what about it? I've been through the whirligig. You fail in this life and in others. Rule Britannia.' She was prudent, however, looking at the failed faces compassionately, shaking her bun, suggesting that perhaps a further session or a Wednesday meeting might be helpful. Sometimes they left her with a bottle of oil, as well as having their palms read spiritually. If a gentleman client was misled by her advertisement she told them 'Readings, nothing physical. Palms only.' Rat oil for them. A hospital was excellent for unquiet spirits and future custom. Spirits loved sick-beds. Geriatric wards were better than this one. How credulous that Copper woman looked. The Doge felt like taking out her teeth and making a face at her. Instead she leaned softly into the brat's cradle. 'My tiny one, my Ginger. The angels must have fancied you. How could they bear to let you go?' On the puny side, but quiet enough. She had no liking for a brat's palm, unmarked by fate or character.

Ruth said some patients went home next day by ambulance. She didn't mind the ward, as long as Logan and the Doge came. The food trays were delicious. Mrs. Copper was a friend already.

'Only if you've somebody at home. At home, you need someone.' Mrs. Copper liked staying. A break from chores and Old Copper. If only she needn't go back.

'Stay,' said Logan. He hadn't made No. 3 ready yet. The birth had filled him with excited restlessness and energy. There was a lot to do. Last night he'd coped with anger, shouting, Leslie leaving. The world had a new direction now, Ruth had had a baby. His life in Ladbroke Grove was finished. He was his brother's keeper, had taken Jordan's place. He'd look after them. Tangerine was providential.

'Rest, my one. Let life regain balance.' With contracted lids the Doge imagined a violet light round Mrs. Copper's head. Gooseberry smoking helped you to see auras. Her cat, short-sighted eyes and her imagination were the Doge's main assets.

After she had kissed Ruth with strong tan-coloured lips the Ward watched her sweep out. She'd bring some potted orange mince next time. Logan put his hand along Ruth's cheek. The adoration he felt astonished him. He'd never felt so moved. The thought of a mother and a baby, his to protect, made him blink. His love had started that morning, in the kitchen when her waters broke. She'd looked so wet and helpless.

Mrs. Copper thought it was ever so moving. The two of them in their cuckoo world, they ought to be alone. A ward was too public, scarcely the place for it, not to mention the nig nurse and her black eyes.

Nurse Asuni asked what the smell was. She flapped her apron. Drain-smells were arch-enemies to hygiene. Normally Mrs. Copper wouldn't open her mouth to a nig but she couldn't resist telling her about the tobacco. A right old stink for round a tiddler, nothing gardeny about it.

Nurse Asuni rolled her eyes.

'You fond of gardens, Ruth?' Mrs. Copper had once seen nasturtiums the colour of Ruth's hair.

'No.'

'Fond of the country?'

'I was never there a lot. I lived with a lady with a garden.' Only for the garden lady she might not hate the memory of her mother so strongly. Her mother taught her fear, walking towards her, smiling, across the frosted grass. A fear of home in Battersea, fear of the sound of her tread across the frosted grass where leaves from the fruit trees fell. Once having got her back her mother left Battersea for good. It was less easy to remember the garden in mid-summer, green, bright with butterflies.

'And Logan? What about him?'

'He liked some parts of country life, he was brought up there.' He'd spoken of the cowslips, sudden storms over the ocean, places with lovely sounding names, Lulworth Cove, Durdle Door, Dancing Ledge. He'd sweet memories along with bitter ones.

'I'm Paddington born and bred. Old Copper is my main complaint.' The country was pretty enough on a day trip, seen behind coach windows, or on the telly. Gardens were for those with money. Growing things, a bit of green, was nice for a tiddler, but for herself Mrs. Copper was past caring. The city was safer. You felt secure with houses round, tall buildings. Jobs, a man to keep you, council places, chip-shops, bingo, were more easy to get in cities. She'd not have met a girl like Ruth in the country. She tried not to envy her. That car, that Logan, that shiny straight hair. Her boobs weren't much to shout about, like buttons compared to her own, whose condition Old Copper was responsible for. Fancy standing starkers for men to paint you. She watched Ruth use her toothbrush, gently buzzing it along her back teeth, her lips closed to prevent the paste leaking. Mrs. Copper longed for thicker hair and better teeth.

Nurse Asuni preferred a mother to feed with the milk that came freely. Bottles were extra work, but Mrs. Cash was little trouble. She warned her not to drink, drinks encouraged lactation. Mrs. Cash's visitors had been most curious, but had been good for Ward morale.

Ruth slept with her myrrh-smelling wrist under her cheek. Mrs. Copper lay facing her. She felt the skinny Arab needed watching.

In the morning the Ward resounded with liquid sounds. Wash basins for bed-patients were dumped onto lockers. Slops competed with the sound of pouring tea, of tea swallowed, of milk sucked from nipple or bottle. Faces were flannelled, hands greased with soap. Nurses poured antiseptic rinse over torn vaginas, cisterns gushed, sluices softly flowed. Mrs. Copper complained of the music. All she could get on her headphones was Debussy's La Mer. Foreign stuff.

'Your love life's o.k. then, Ruth?'

'I told you about my husband leaving. Logan is my brother-in-law.'

'You need a man round Christmas time.' Though Mrs. Copper was past caring. Without a man in the home, Christmas wouldn't be quite the thing, but in the Ward you could make paper chains. The nurses, even the nig ones, were extra kind and no one felt left out. She asked if Ruth's lady friend was coming again that afternoon.

'Primrose, my girl-friend, is.

'Primrose? That's a pretty name. Is she an artist too?' She watched Ruth buzz her brush again. Such a pretty noise.

'We were at school. Then she was secretary at the place I worked.' She didn't really want Primrose anywhere near the Ward.

Her arrival caused another stir. Real affluence was rare in the district, real money had an air. Anyone could flash a fancy nightie, or talcum from a pricey tin while they talked about a win on Ernie. Real wealth was different. It was a way of moving, the way you ignored people, didn't care. Primrose knew they stared at her, she ignored everybody. She'd got what she wanted, nothing else existed. She bought gifts for poor Ruth stuck in a ward full of the working class, stuck in a world she wanted no part of.

As each head turned its owner felt ashamed of the bunches of michaelmas daisies, cheap fruit squashes, gifts from their working loved ones. Primrose made an ordinary apple or orange a poor thing. Her coat was chinchilla. She tipped her nose up as if to avoid smelling them. Her size was frightening, her hands were big as mutton legs, holding pink and yellow roses. Mrs. Copper had to stop herself squealing. She batched the newspapers on her locker together.

'I couldn't resist buying something rather special for you, Ruth.' Primrose put the roses and some sparkling wrapped chocolates on the locker. She said she was fond of dolls, unwrapping a bulky parcel. Mrs. Copper couldn't help herself from giving a groan of desire. Ruth's lower scrubbed teeth dropped, her mouth stayed open. The doll was so obnoxious she could say nothing.

'You see, it's adjustable,' Primrose explained. You altered it to any size. From infant size, it grew. You squeezed and its complicated inner mechanism changed, increasing or decreasing to what you wanted. Its trunk and limbs coordinated. Spare parts were in another box, tiny teeth, re-shapable lips, nails, a variety of wigs. It could echo its owner's whim. Mrs. Copper groaned again. Money wrought miracles. Primrose could spend a hundred and fifteen pounds on a plaything for a friend, to say nothing of the extras. The price was on the box. She watched Primrose shaping it, a look of holy power on her face, her great hands slowly kneading. The Ward was silent.

'Look, Ruth. Tiny, newly born. I'll put a bonnet on it, shall I?'

'It's wonderful. Don't you want to look at Tangerine, though. She's going to wake.'

'She's super, yes. Look, real lambswool.'

'But, Primrose, look at her. She's so lovely. I didn't have a bad time with her. I quite enjoyed it.' Primrose was wicked not to look. Ruth didn't want that present, she wanted Primrose to go.

'Was it all right? See the toes. The skin turns paler if you want, see the pink hands.'

Mrs. Copper could have wept. The most exquisite gift money could buy and Ruth didn't bother, could only think of her ordinary tiddler and its birth. Primrose was a benefactress and Ruth behaved as if the doll was from Woolworths.

Ruth said that her baby was the quietest in the Ward, as well as the most beautiful. Mrs. Copper's was nice too.

'Super, yes. Look, a milk bottle, little toilet things.'

'I wish you'd look, Prim. I know your present is amazing but Tangerine has just been born.'

All the Ward was looking. Nurse Asuni said the doll was love-worthy enough to put in the crib under the Ward tree. Would Primrose like some Horlicks? Hot drinks time, but not for Mrs. Cash, not too much liquid intake. Milk drinks for all except non-breast-feeders. Eyes stared at Primrose and her doll, round, watchful over the rims of their cups. She sipped with one hand, continuing to caress the doll with the other.

'Why not let Mrs. Copper see it, Prim. Mrs. Copper, meet Primrose.' The way they all drooled could only mean that the whole ward in-cluding Nurse Asuni were maternally frustrated. Their real babies weren't enough for them, they wanted illusion, they wanted childish freedom, to play without involvement.

'One moment,' Primrose adjusted the limbs again, not looking at Mrs. Copper. The doll gave a spasm, thickened, lengthened, its cheeks swelling as if the tongue were bursting. A pat, a little prod, the doll became a toddler. Mrs. Copper stretched a craving hand.

The patients sighed with envy. This was real child-rearing, the fun without the agony. Mrs. Copper was oblivious to everyone, forgot all but the present. Forgot the time Old Copper let her have it with his boot, the time the pram broke in Shillington Street, forgot twins, forgot scabies, forgot the tiddler climbing into the clothes spinner.

This was living.

At last Primrose looked at Ruth. 'Pete and I have been talking about you. Have you told Jordan?'

'Jordan? Why tell him?'

'He should be footing bills. Be sensible, Ruth, get your priorities right.'

'Tangerine is my priority. She's all I worry about.' And later Logan would come again.

'Be practical. You need money.' The thin-faced tart was loco, staring into the cradle, staring at her toothbrush. And not a word of thanks for her presents. Money and love went hand in glove, that no one could dispute. It was the essential truth. Jordan should be sleuthed. What were lawcourts for? That arty carry on, scribbling in diaries, Logan, would get Ruth nowhere.

Ruth thought of Logan's gentleness, his eyes and hands. She didn't need Jordan any more than she needed her mother.

'He did father your tiddler, Ruth. Remember that. You are obliged to your Mum as well.' Mrs. Copper pressed the doll to her cheek.

'My mother gave me a rotten childhood. Jordan deserted me. What do I owe either of them?' She'd see that Tangerine was wrapped in love, maternal and paternal. She'd die for her.

Mrs. Copper rocked, eyelids drooping. Ruth ought to bury the past. Impossibilities didn't drop from heaven, you had to buy them. You got money and you purchased. Where would the world be without money? She wouldn't mind a sight of that house in Weybridge.

'Think how much a child costs, Ruth. The bare necessities.' How dare the tart turn up her nose at the doll. She only deserved the rat-run market populated by blacks, deserved to be deserted. She should be jailed.

'Have you seen Logan's car, Primrose? The purple one. A car's a handy thing for birthing. Got tiddlers of your own?'

Primrose didn't answer. Common person, daring to intrude, snatching the doll, contaminating it. She told Ruth she'd said what she had come to say. Before she went away she opened the chocolates, crossly forking a few soft-centred ones into her mouth with the little fork, provided for hygiene. It angered her to have spent money on the tart. Mrs. Copper had no right to touch the doll or ask impertinent questions.

62

Her chinchilla coat left fresh wafts of affluence in its wake as she lumbered out of the Ward. A millionaire smell, the mothers agreed, discussing her afterwards. They'd never forget her. Nurse Asuni thought of her in connection with the League of Friends, made sure she got a leaflet. Donations were appreciated so near the festive season.

'Care for a read of my *Mirror*, Ruth?'

In the evening Logan turned the doll over unbelievingly. Distasteful, vulgar, as vulgar as the giver. And yet he couldn't help being curious. How did it work? For technical ingenuity it was first-class. He'd like to strip it down. His third eye blinked inside, envisaging parts of this doll included in the new construction. This was important, a vital link. No object was valueless in art, no idea should be rejected without consideration. Primrose might be shallow, her friendship valueless; the concept of her gift was shattering. From Hong Kong, he imagined. He couldn't wait to dismantle it. He'd use the rubber hands and other intricate parts. Ruth must look after it. Was it necessary to let all the Ward play with it?

By the time she was ready to leave, everybody had had their turn at it, played lovingly with the doll. Every mother except Ruth kissed and fondled it. They'd never forget the beautiful inflatable doll.

Mrs. Copper was overwhelmed to have the long-stemmed pink and yellow roses, the chocolate box, untouched except for the few Primrose had forked into her mouth.

6

NURSE Asuni's last words were a reminder to watch her fluid intake. Mrs. Cash should understand, too, that unpleasant smells could harm a tiny child. She flapped her apron for the last time out of the window, gave a final sigh. She'd miss Mrs. Cash's visitors. She'd miss the buzzing of her toothbrush and her quiet ways. She'd been no bother. They came in fat, they went out flat, they rarely gave you thanks, especially if your face was black. Producing thriving babies from mothers who forgot you, or slandered you to your face, was thankless. You went on smiling, waiting, despite Mrs. Copper and her kind. Black people could afford to wait, kindness and patience were inbred. Mrs. Cash had thanked her nicely, Mrs. Cash was the kind worth waiting for.

Mrs. Copper sniffed a tear back. The five days had been spent in intimacy. Affections of the heart and life-secrets had been swapped. It was easy to confide when you were unlikely to meet again. Mrs. Copper said that they were ships that pass in the night. She'd think of Ruth each time she saw red hair, remember the girl who wore funny clothes, wrote in a diary and brushed her teeth electrically. Her new tiddler would put a tether on her, Ruth wouldn't live so chancily. Consideration was worth the Bank of England, her Logan was exceptional. She'd watch for purple cars. She'd rather sweep chimneys than go back to Old Copper. Pownde-Welling – there was a name to envy. She took down Ruth's address, just in case. She might pay the Doge Lady a visit one day. That goosegog smoke was calming.

Tangerine was like taking a present home after a holiday. Logan put the soft-topped case and the mechanical doll into the back of the Rolls. After the heat of the Ward the cold was invigorating. Ruth licked her teeth happily. The wheels squashed the slush flatter into the gutters. Tangerine looked pretty in her new brown outdoor shawl. She had been sorry to leave Mrs. Copper. Her stay in hospital had altered her life. She wouldn't swap with anyone. She felt elated, driving the familiar roads again with Logan, turning again into the Market, seeing the snow still heaped on the window ledges of the Emporium. She could pity Primrose, childless in that dreadful house. She pitied her because she had no interest in others. Miss Chips had failed to teach her compassion. In the Ward the mothers came to sit on Ruth's bed, told her about their hopes and fears. They all thought it shameful that Jordan let her down. But husbands did that quite a lot. It was rotten about her mother too. They understood. Drink was a deadener. Everyone died of something. Death was Time's executioner, they nodded wisely. Where did Ruth get those shifts? From an Indian? Nigs and Indians weren't well thought of on the whole. Some quite liked Nurse Asuni though. In spite of Grammar School Ruth was still one of them, they'd talked, accepted her.

'Who are you thinking about?' Logan had worked hard, re-wiring the flat, plastering, rawlplugging. He longed to see the two orange heads against the woollen kitchen curtains. They were so valuable. The smell of soap, urine, milk and new wool fascinated him. He'd started the framework of his new construction. He kept thinking about it. Ruth said she was thinking of the difference between Mrs. Copper and Primrose. Anything Mrs. Copper gave, even a read of her *Mirror*, was given from the heart.

It was Logan who saw the cloaked child. He recognised the dribbling vacant look from Ruth's description. The skin round her mouth was sore from wet and the weather. She was looking into the Doge's mirror, turning round to look into the Rolls. She stared at Tangerine with pitch-dark eyes. He was relieved that Ruth, busy settling the brown shawl, didn't see her. He would say nothing about her. Ruth must stay calm and quiet. She had her child to think of. The city was full of neglected cases. People rotted, uncared-for, like the buildings. Few cared about the irredeemable. The black-haired child in ragged clothes, nodding her head, looked hopeless. He'd always cared for physical appearances. Soon it would be time for Tangerine's bottle.

They drew up outside the garage. Ruth shivered. Tangerine was sopping. Back in the Ward Mrs. Copper would be telling her successor about life in Paddington and Old Copper. She wondered if Nurse Asuni and the other mothers would miss her. The trays had been hot and filling.

'I'm tired. Suddenly.'

He said she must go in quickly. She must rest.

'Don't bring the doll in.'

He said he'd put it in the garage, out of sight. He told her that wealth was hard to part with. That Mrs. Copper owned little and was generous. Primrose was as materialistic as his father who had a text over his desk. 'Dawn breaks, death takes. Prepare with Cash & Whaler.' When Uncle Whaler died his father wept, but secretly re-joiced that there'd be less profit-sharing. Ruth looked lovely, different without make-up, cuddling her baby in the brown shawl. He'd asked her once where she had been fostered, the home with the garden. She couldn't remember, two bus distances away from Battersea. He settled Tangerine on the divan. They'd soon adjust to the new rou-tine. Ruth nodded. A family now. You said 'We' instead of 'I'. Her father and her mother never had been 'we'. He used to beg her to jack her job in, models weren't well thought of. For the joys of 'we' Mrs. Copper gave her freedom. Primrose bought her passage to the state of 'we' via Miss Chips' School.

'Logan, I feel very peculiar.' They'd said you should take care. That you could haemorrhage. Mrs. Copper's varicosed legs came from doing too much too soon.

'You're bound to feel the change-over from hospital to home. It's the adjustment. You should lie down. I'll do your shoes again.'

She nodded. She sat at the same chair where his hands had been drenched earlier by waters from his brother's child. Unstrapping now. Different now. The child had come and they were 'we'. He'd taken the plastic anklet from Tangerine to keep in his wallet. The table was set with a table-cloth. The sink was clean. No smell of mice or joss sticks, but Dettol and green soap. Different, neater, clean. Only the herb jars and the dried plants were unchanged. She hoped he'd never hear the things they'd called her. 'Art School Bike', 'Push-Over'. She wished she'd had a happy adolescence. When did adolescence stop for good?

'I'm so cold. Is it really finished between you and Leslie?'

'Yes. It never was really right.' Not from the beginning. As interest in sculpture increased, his absorption in Leslie waned. Then Ruth appeared and life changed. He said he'd run the bath for her.

She lay in the steam, watching it rise. The towels and paintwork were the same dull colour as Logan's eyes. She could make out the branches of the pear trees, snow-thickened in the dark outside, the top twigs spread like fingers. The houses backing onto the garden were rarely lit. At night you sometimes heard strange pipe music, the laughter of coloured people, uncontrolled, sustained, but the occupants remained unseen. She was in Logan's hands, a man with bath-mat-coloured eyes, who'd packed in Leslie and loved sculpture. Beyond the pear trees and the jungle laughter was a market of people taking their lives earnestly, all hoping for improvement. Wheeling and dealing, football pools, drink, music, a baby were all part of the scheme of things, hope of improvement. She picked the blood flecks from her thighs, spattered still. This was her first bath; the hospital care had been basic. Patients attended to the niceties themselves. She rubbed the Doge's oil into the stretched skin of her stomach. She rubbed old skin away from the cracks between her toes. She worked the flannel thoroughly around both ears before putting her head back, floating her hair in the aromatic water. Her ears made bubbling sounds. Sometimes she still wished she had practised the violin. The garden lady tried to teach her carols, 'We Three Kings' and 'I Saw Three Ships'. You needed patience and discipline, hours of enduring ugly sounds before anything worthwhile came. She hummed quietly. Her eyes and nose broke the surface of the water. Logan had put a glass shelf over her head for baby things, and some of the dried leaves for decoration. She could see the dark seeds through the transparency of the honesty pods. Steam ran down in droplets collecting on the stalks and in the bulrush prickles. The end of her old life, the beginning of another. The water sucked at her hairline. She felt melancholy.

Logan pushed the door. 'I've fed her. No trouble at all. Primrose rang while you were washing. Was it wise to wash your hair?' He handed warmed towels to her. He couldn't disguise his dislike of Primrose, in spite of her interesting doll. Her contempt for Ruth was obvious, he couldn't understand her continued interest in a worn-out friendship. But he'd talked courteously on the telephone, given her news of the home-coming. He'd put a bottle in Ruth's bed. The mattress on the floor was excellent, would help strengthen her tired back. He liked spare furnishing himself, economy of possessions. Possessions could rule your life. The way you lived affected the quality of your work. Life should be kept simple, he agreed with Ruth. As far as possible he liked objects in the home to be functional. He disliked untidiness. He'd put the goatskin on the floor under Tangerine's basket. The mattress had a dark green eiderdown tucked round it. Ruth mustn't get chilled. She got under the eiderdown and slept.

She dreamed of somewhere far away. A garden, safe. Not safe, threatening. Was it the garden lady calling her? There were fruit trees, high branches containing hidden lemons, citrus fruits. Fruit juice dribbled down her face, juice from the lemons. The garden lady's voice turned deeper. 'My one, you are the chosen. My one, you, you.' The fruit fell, turning into money, hitting her, a rain of coins.

'Come on. Ruth, Ruth.'

'What is it? Is Tangerine all right?'

'You were moaning. Wake up. She's asleep.' He hated the sound of sleepers in distress. Jordan, when they'd shared a room as boys, had shouted, ground his teeth. He felt ashamed in those days for hating Jordan and his own inadequacy. When faced with dreamers you felt powerless.

'I dreamed. Awful.' Her face was wet with sweat, the drops running like tears. She hadn't cried for years, tears served no purpose, they changed nothing. She'd not cried since she left the garden.

'You must eat something. You've slept for hours.'

'What time is it?'

'Nearly eleven'. He'd given Tangerine her night bottle. Ruth hadn't heard the Doge knock, had missed the sight of her cat looped round her neck, its front paws tucked into the buttonhole. The Doge brought liquorice bootlaces. She often glided round the market, chewing at night, her cat wound like a warm collar round her.

'You're staying, Logan? Are you going to stay?'

'Of course. I couldn't leave you. You need me.'

He came back with a tray. He wore faded clean pyjamas, his hair in spikes like kindling wood. He looked younger. His long shins poked from the hems when he sat on the mattress. He wasn't hirsute like Jordan. Jordan's toes had hair on them. Her dream faded as he described the Doge's visit. He gave her the bag of bootlaces. He admired the old lady, living as she pleased, not caring. It took courage to be eccentric. He sensed that Ruth was steely underneath. Inside, she was no victim.

She moved her legs to make room for the tray, bumping against

68

him, a flattened place to balance it. She wondered if the green eider-down had covered him and Leslie, if Logan had poured tea for her too and made her plates of toast. He'd remembered that Ruth hated sugar. The butter was salty, delicious, running down her fingers. He made her eat each square, hot, nicely browned. She felt his long smooth toes, cold against her own. The dream was gone.

'Don't feel you have to stay. I can manage.'

He didn't answer, touching her cheek. The way he touched, his hand hard-skinned yet soft, was like her father touching her neck, to check enquiringly that her latchkey was round her neck before school, not being able to rely on her mother being home. Her father had packed sandwiches. Logan stroked her, not like her father, intrusively, touching, stroking her with salty-tasting fingers, his mat-coloured eyes watching her. He knew her childhood had been miserable. He knew she would survive. Tangerine was in the basket on the goatskin by them.

His 'Fruition' would be three times life-size. He knew which parts of the old fruit machine he'd use, which parts of the doll. Other objects, a purple hardback, a fish, some plaited hair he was still considering—objects of differing shape and texture. Ideas energised each time he looked at Ruth. Money didn't come into it, had no bearing on real love or real endeavour. Her neck was so long. Eyes in his fingertips he felt it again.

'I'm still bleeding.' The smell of milk and blood was characteristic, intrinsic to birth, clung to you, though she had no breast milk. His jacket smelled of instant milk mixture. She liked the smell.

'Of course. Trust me.'

The toes of his left foot rubbed her calf, new-scrubbed from her bath. His knees were warm now. She felt him. They would fondle, touch, kiss, remembering her blood. His kisses were long, getting longer, remembering her blood. She wanted to make him happy, to feel wanted, he had something sad, something out of reach about him, and he was gentle, remembering her blood. He touched her nipples, moving to her thighs. She was the world to him, he esteemed her highly, she and his work were his salvation. And so they clung, remembering her blood.

At dawn she woke, remembering the blood that would continue to flow up to three weeks. She got up quietly, leaving him and her

69

child to sleep. He would move in with her. Her future, truly shared at last, seemed winged. They'd live as life should be lived, considering each other, with a shared aim. She didn't put the light on. In the grey-white light outside she saw a youth crouching by the garage. The Close street light switched out after she'd seen. He was with the cloaked market child, his arm round her, their faces raised towards the bedroom where she watched. He wore a leather coat. Pressed together they made the shape of a preying animal, menacing. She would be calm. She would ignore them. She would say nothing.

Later, when Logan was up, he was shocked to find his old fruit machine had been smashed. The garage had been broken into, someone had smashed the glass. The loganberries, plums and other fruit alignments had been smashed into. The handle was cracked in two. As well, the tyres of the purple Rolls had been slashed, the chassis scratched. He minded the damage to his one-armed bandit more than the Rolls. He looked shaken.

'Who was it? I saw somebody outside. Who could it have been?'

He didn't answer, tightening his rather full lips, peering again at the machine. He'd planned to dismember, not desecrate it. The Rolls could be put right. The machine had been outraged. He picked the broken piece of handle from the floor.

'I did see someone. A youth. A youth in a leather coat. He was with that little girl, that girl I told you about, who scared me. It was early. Dark.'

He looked at the machine again, ruined in the window. Outside snow was falling again. He spoke in a strained voice, his face turned from her. 'A leather coat? It was . . . I'm afraid that it was Leslie.'

'Leslie? How could it be her? This was a boy, a young man in a leather coat, I told you.'

'It was Leslie.'

'But . . . a man? I had no idea. It was a man. Why didn't you tell me?'

He looked out at the garden, at the snow and the pear trees, his hand still holding the broken handle. He looked trapped, his eyes darker. Leslie was over, an episode. The relationship was never based on feeling, not real feeling. It was over. His eyes implored. He loved her. Leslie and he had quarrelled constantly. Leslie was spiteful. He'd done damage for revenge. That part of his life was over, he belonged to her now, could she understand? Jordan had failed her, he wanted to support, console and love her, couldn't she understand?

She'd been fooled, that's what she minded most. Why hadn't he told her? She was open-minded, why hadn't he said? What upset her was his lack of trust. She trusted him, why hadn't he trusted her?

His lack of trust upset her more than anything.

'I'm sorry. I was going to. You see . . . I'm not . . .I'm not like that. I'm not gay. Leslie was something I had to get out of my system.' He found explanation nearly impossible. He wanted to stand high, unshakable in her esteem. He wasn't unmanly. And he must have her trust, always.

'Is that why Jordan wouldn't talk about you? Did he know?'

'He guessed. He was disgusted. He didn't understand. Leslie couldn't last.' He'd been something Logan had to work through, a kind of delayed adolescence. He loved Ruth with a man's love. She did believe that? He was normal.

'I do believe it.' What was normal? Her father suffering her mother long after love died, suffering without recompense? Primrose and Pete's obsession with themselves and monetary gain? The Doge who loved her dead, charging for what she said they told her? Megalomaniac Jordan unable to endure family responsibilities? Mrs. Copper enduring Old Copper for a doubtful security? Everyone she knew fell far short of the Garden Lady's principle. 'Be kindly and affectionate to one another.'

'I'm not proud about it.' Neither could he control it at the time. He'd been insane over Leslie, a sickness that had to burn itself out. He loved Ruth protectively and utterly. He loved the way an artist did, they'd love and live for his work, for each other and the child.

'But why not say? I've told you things.' Not everything. Not how she'd lived, promiscuously. She'd hate him to see old diaries, her casual non-involvements, one-night stands.

'I didn't want you to think I was like Jordan, unable to sustain a relationship. I was going to tell. We must have no secrets.' He'd intended to tell everything. Of how the thought of Leslie sickened him now, especially after this garage episode. Leslie had discredited him as man and artist. It would take care and skill to restore his one-armed bandit. The window by the passenger seat of the Rolls was shattered. The city attracted flotsam.

71

'What do you mean "delayed adolescence?" '

He spoke about his involvement with his family, the unhealthiness of outlook, the love-hate tie with Jordan, their feelings about the business. Then he told her about the fat girl on the day of the washed-up corpse. He'd pretended to himself that Leslie's mind attracted him. It was his body, his hard brown body that erased the fat girl from his mind. He'd desired him. He'd soon found out his spite, the triviality of his nature. Pretended love led quickly to indifference. Leslie was stupid, greedy, had demanded expensive leather clothing. Jordan had never seen him, had never seen his good looks. Leslie mocked. Logan had wanted him for a model, but he wouldn't pose.

'Why did you rent Jordan's garage?'

'For quiet. For peace away from Leslie. It was handy.' Old ties were difficult to break, dislike and closeness interdependent. To be physically near, yet not speaking, suited the brothers. He knew that Jordan had deluded himself about his writing, the way he'd bragged. But he understood the desire to leave something behind, to record something personal. The pull of brotherhood remained. Because of it Logan had Ruth now.

'Why was that little girl with him?'

'I don't know. He never mentioned any family.' He'd put a heavy padlock on the doors, make it foolproof. Leslie would soon find others to keep him in leather clothes and idleness.

'You should have told me about that drowned body thing.'

'I hate the sea.' The sea was cruel. The sea brought Cash & Whaler trade, topped up the yearly quota. Deep water washed up fat women.

The Doge wanted to hear all about it. Who had battered their jalopy? Paint all spoiled, the window out. She swallowed a scrap of bootlace. What was the girlie wearing? Was Ruth sure it was the same child, the child in the brown cloak? Rule Britannia. It was well-known that poltergeists liked purple. It was upsetting to see her fruit machine. Ruined. She touched the lever sadly. The citrus fruits had got the worst of it. She wished now she hadn't parted with it. Obviously it buzzed with vibrations. Er . . . she didn't want to pry, but were they sure the young man was Logan's . . . flatmate? They were? She got it. Young persons crossed could be most nasty. Love soured before it rotted. People found it where they could. She'd found none herself, no physical love in this existence. Her loyal Genoese

72

sent messages into her ear, she didn't complain. She managed. Oddments and jobments, a bit of buy and sell, her palmistry and meetings
kept her afloat. Money kept the world aspin, not only love. She
peered again. Could human hands have left scratches of such depth?
How many thousand supplicants had paid coins, pulled that handle
hopefully. Which pier turnstiles, amusement arcades had it stood
in? Too late to think of using it for her Wednesdays now, as background atmosphere. Too late. She nodded as he explained about his
plan. A work of art, part of his sculpting work? A Christmas carving
did he mean, updated?

She offered more liquorice to Ruth who shook her head. Sweets
were bad for the teeth, especially that black stuff, though she didn't
like to offend the kind Doge. 'We wondered, Doge, if you would
like to spend the day here with us. It will be quite quiet. We're
having a goose. And Logan is putting a tree in the kitchen.'

'Ta. I will.'

He made decorations of blown glass for the tree. Christmas was
on a Wednesday. He glued the branches before spraying them with
ground glass, leaving the undersides shadowy. Glass-tipped, each
tinsel-threaded bough was delicate against the whiteness outside.
'We three' for Christmas. Three was not a crowd, it was just right.
They'd have no secrets sealed from each other. At night they lay
together, her yellow slitty eyes close to his grey ones. Relationships
thrived on truth. She told him about the Institute and her old reputation, how she'd been so isolated. How infatuation warmed you, you
were connected for a time, until it died and you were isolated again.
Isolation and feeling worthless were constituent. He told her about
Leslie, about Jordan's bounced cheque and visiting the Librarian
who'd looked so sick at the mention of him. Tangerine was pretty
as an angel. Primrose sent a card that played a carol when you
pressed. They'd have champagne. They'd have surprises. Ruth looked
at the tree a lot. She thought he ought to do his sculpture all the
time. His work would sell anywhere. He told her that selling was
not the important thing, what mattered was the endeavour. The
journeying counted, not arriving. He was so happy with her. On
Christmas Eve he put up silver lights like a canopy. From the mattress
they could watch it, a cascade, warming, lighting them. He'd in-
stalled extra power points. It was the longest snow-fall for ten years.

Tangerine had eyes like Ruth's, staring at the lights after her bottles. They'd done a lot of shopping.

In the morning she felt something rustle over her waking foot under the green eiderdown, a scratching like cloth tearing. She lay rigid, feeling the old childish fear of something, someone coming to grab her.

'You said you never had a stocking. So, go on, open it.'

Grown up, a mother on a mattress, not a scared child in Battersea. She had a stocking and, outside, bells were ringing. He'd got up early, lit the oven for the goose. It was early and she had a stocking. Grown-up, but he'd put in childish things to please her. Nuts in the toe, a tangerine, a silver threepenny-piece, a glass Santa Claus. There were some leather slippers, curious ear-rings. She opened each thing carefully, put on the slippers and the ear-rings The room smelled nice, myrrh and the beginnings of the goose cooking, richly stuffed. He took a smaller box from his pillow. The gold had worn thin. Under the pearls you could read 'Love'. The pearls were set flatly, a gypsy setting, he explained, for comfortable wear. It fitted her third finger. Pearls were said to be unlucky, but he said not if you wore them always. They had talked of marriage. If Jordan wasn't traced after two years, divorce was short work. It was convenient that Tangerine was already legally registered Cash. Perhaps Jordan really had left the country like Gauguin.

'I believe in your work, Logan. The construction will succeed. I'll help. I love you. I believe in you.'

'You're the loveliest thing that ever happened. Always remember I love you.'

A slipper fell from her outstretched toe, an ear-ring rolled into her hair. Washed by their sweat, semen and saliva, and the crushed tangerine, they moved lovingly. Loving slowly like underwater creatures while her hair wound round, wet in the water, the nuts, the threepenny, the earrings, the sharp pips of the fruit pressed their limbs like shells. She would be Mrs. Logan Cash, a silver future ahead of her.

The Doge's gift was her crystal ball to prop their bedroom door. The smell of goose got stronger. They'd put a lemon in to absorb excess grease. He told her vegetarianism was silly, unless you abstained from conviction. She ought to eat more. Her arms were a little too thin. He slept again while she watched the snow, watched her pearl ring in the light, watched the Christmas lights in the Doge's crystal. The goose made spittings in its foil wrapping. She'd look after her hands for the new ring, have more baths, eat more.

He said a child absorbed surroundings. He put Tangerine under the tree, where she could sense festivity and love. Her basket fitted nicely under the lower branches. She was a small baby. Logan lit some angel chimes. The gold figures revolved slowly over the flames' heat.

The Doge wore her cat which she removed carefully before lighting a gooseberry puff. 'My ones, the Comps. Now, Puss, down. Stop sniffing.' Puss always sniffed when he sensed vibrations. Rule Britannia. She was partial to her own home-brew, had brought some for them, never mind champagne. What news? Anything unusual?

'There are no spirits here, Doge. Do you take sugar?'

'No, ta. I meant . . . er . . . any further sightings?'

'Oh Doge, not that again. It's Christmas. See, I'm wearing your gilt fish.'

'I only meant have you seen Leslie or the child, that's all, my one.'

'Of course not. Look at the table.'

The Doge brought sandal wood biscuits as well. She'd have a touch, a slice or two of the breast. She didn't ordinarily eat goose. How nice her crystal looked. Logan spooned gravy into Baby's mouth. Puss sucked giblets under the stove. The gold angels tinkle tinkled in the centre of the table. The kitchen was a changed place now, since Ruth first lay there with Jordan. The Doge crunched a small bone thoughtfully. She'd brought some sugar coins, gold-wrapped, for the brat. She hadn't got a lead on Jordan's whereabouts. Her crystal clouded since her eyes got bad, she'd wanted them to have it. They'd been kind, giving her a copy of 'The Tarot Made Easy' to mark the day.

'Doge, I want to show you what Logan gave me. Will you come to the bedroom?'

'Ta, I will.'

It was the happiest dinner all of them had ever eaten. The sky was darkening, a yellow heaviness. They pushed Tangerine further into the overhanging branches to lie in brilliance, a net of love. The Doge pulled her cat away again. A cat was so hot. She followed

75

Ruth into the bedroom, sitting on the mattress, having covered her thin calves with her skirt. She looked at the things admiringly.

'Let me see the ring again, my one.' Logan had specially asked her advice. She'd found the pearl one for him. She'd guessed the size perfectly. So suitable for Pisceans.

'I'll wear it all the time. I'll put gloves on for washing-up.'

'No need specially, my one.'

'Arrrrrgh.'

'Get out. Get back. Devil. Get out of that.'

There was a sound of hitting. From the kitchen came the sound of hits, of claws hitting the floorboards, of snarls, miaows, bangs, hits. Logan was hitting Puss.

While the Doge had been examining presents in the bedroom her Puss had crept out, had sneaked under the divan, found the old doll wrapped in brown paper. Had dragged it across the floor and jumped into the cradle. Logan hit it several times before it would move from Tangerine's feet. It crouched under the table, tearing at the doll's body. Scraps of clothing lay under its mouth. Sawdust, hair, ripped limbs were round it. It stared up, part of the doll's face still in its mouth. Painted doll's eyes showed through a cluster of whiskers.

'My one, my Puss. He meant nothing. Come Puss, apologise.'

'She's all right, Logan. Tangerine hasn't woken. Don't worry, Doge, it's all right.'

Safe under the silver web of branches Tangerine still slept.

7

SHE took Tangerine back to the Ward. She wanted advice and re-assurance from Mrs. Copper who was experienced in birthing, tiddler-raising. Mrs. Copper would know. The Ward might know of her address in Paddington. Strangers lay now in their old beds, swapping secrets, comparing lives. Nurse Asuni gave her a sparkling smile. Usually they faded from her mind, once out of her hands she avoided thinking about them. Mrs. Cash had been different. Her looks, her visitors, her gratitude when she'd said goodbye had been most heart-warming. The Registrar would probably help her, would have a record of past patients. What was the trouble? Her baby looked healthy. Not large, but wiry. At six months she should be taken regularly to the Clinic. What were Health Visitors for?

Logan was patient. He agreed with the Health Visitor, Ruth was fussing needlessly. She worried daily, wringing her hands over Tangerine's development. She had no interests apart from worrying and writing in her diary. Instead of being thankful for a quiet baby she agonised. Why didn't she wheel her in the pram he'd bought? The market people would like to see her, everybody loved babies. He felt so blessed, couldn't Ruth feel the same? He'd never had such purpose, his own family to support as well as his art. What was wrong, truly?

'I worry that there's something they haven't spotted. She's so passive, Logan. She must see someone.'

'She eats. She puts on weight. Relax.'

'She sleeps so much. She must be unhappy.'

'Why? Why must she?'

'I'm sure she never wanted to be born.' She'd read of young babies suffering from depression.

'It's you who are depressed, Ruth. And no one chooses to be born.'

He wished she would remember that he loved her, put her first. Low spirits went with lack of self-regard. Since Christmas she had drooped round like a sleep-walker. She never wore anything but black. She hadn't posed as they had planned, though his 'Fruition' was well on the way just the same. Each night after he'd finished his maintenance and repairing, after he'd seen them both to bed he went downstairs again to work, the work that really mattered to him. Her seated figure, square, angular, would be cast in iron. She sat splay-legged, hands held forward, ready to catch the emerging child. Because she hadn't posed, the piece had become more surrealistic than he'd originally planned. He'd incorporated the doll's components as intended. The projecting child, a foetal shape in glass, had inflatable hands attached by wire springs. Various wheels and joints lent quality, suggested the idea of birth, a mood rather than a statement. Except for the eyes, her and the child's features were vague. The upper part of the fruit machine was set into her thorax. Long strands of rope fell freely from her head. Her eyes were orange perspex. The glassy shape between her thighs would have fine twine on its pate and silvery eyes. When finished it would measure seven feet by four. Fresh details kept coming to him. The early sketches, done upstairs when she had been big, had triggered it, had turned the key. He wanted an anticipatory effect, suspense before manifestation. Ruth's lit-up Christmas look was gone. She was as moon-faced, as hand-twisting, as Lady Macbeth. The Doge didn't come as often, no cheering visits since her Puss had died. She didn't go round the market chewing liquorice, but crept silently, wearing a look of tragedy, her neck cold without its cat covering. There'd been no more mention of Leslie.

Recently Ruth had taken to rising from her mattress, to lean over the cradle, sleep muttering, before he led her back to him. She wouldn't remember in the morning. Breakfast, feeding them, was hurried because of his customers who needed him too. Mending, restoring went on in spite of trade booms or depressions. If visiting a specialist would help Ruth they'd better see the doctor about it. She was tortured. They would go.

'The Rolls is living up to her maiden trip. You'd never know she'd been beaten up.' He reminded her how worried she'd been then, yet how joyfully they'd come home with Tangerine. It would happen again this time. After they'd seen the specialist they'd feel joy again. Dr. Greanbach would make her see sense. Why must she cross bridges unnecessarily? She sat clutching the child as if they were about to hit a reef. She'd become as inturned as Primrose if she didn't watch it. He wished she had made more of herself for the appointment. She looked half-drunk.

'That dead cat might have harmed her. Might have done something. How do we know?'

The Doge had shaken her greasy bun over Tangerine's palm, had not been reassuring. The cat's demise had been an unexpected and shattering blow for her.

Logan said the cat had died of an infected rat-bite. Ruth was far too fanciful.

'I'm sure the Doge suspects something is wrong.'

'The Doge has gone to wrack.' She had lost custom since the cat's death. Bits of her mince got into her oils. The new cat spat at customers. People didn't want a tragic face staring over their palms, they wanted understanding, knowledge. She dressed carelessly, only going out at night to the Indian's alley to poke notes under his door. Smells from her kitchen were worse.

'Supposing they pull Fyste Close down?'

Logan had written to complain of the buildings round them. Bricks fell. Broken pipes were an invitation to vermin. The area was scheduled for development. The topic was discussed with unease in the market. Nothing was definitely known. In summer the Indian music, eastern revelry and laughter was louder in the night. He said they'd be re-housed, it wouldn't be disastrous. Why anticipate? They were all right. Eventually they'd have to move somewhere more spacious.

They passed the Indian's alley. He showed no sign of occupation. The brown-skinned figures flitting back and forth were the only proof of his existence. The Doge's intimacy was based on correspondence. The market people said strange shrieks sounded from the alley sometimes, shrieks like an animal in pain, unearthly. Little by little the regulars, stall-holders who'd worked there for generations, were moving to new premises. They spoke of the luck of the market running out. Places soon went down. Their stalls were taken quickly enough by Indians, or Asians with slitty eyes. There was no lack of commerce going on. They drove past the Classic Cinema showing 'How to Make a Million'.

79

'Logan, did your mother die having you? Can you remember her?'

'No.' He didn't want to dwell on it. Illness, death, were better not discussed. Ruth would bankrupt herself emotionally if she dwelled on death. Had she noticed the buds uncurling in the thin sun? A lorry in front of them contained sacks of broccoli, spring greens and imported apples. His inner eye would remember.

'Yes. A green mist. Like when I first came here.' Two winters and two summers ago when she'd looked out from Jordan's oak-framed bed, seen green leaves and her life beginning. The home was right now, bare, quiet, muted. Tangerine was the only worry. 'I do want to get back to posing. Loving, living like we used. The thing is I just feel so damned miserable.'

He stroked her, thinking about the light, the light on Tangerine's hair, light red with greenish undertones, the greens of the vegetables, green leaves, the property of light, determining shape, reflection. His work would be affected if she stayed permanently sad. Art should disturb, it should elate, excite the participant, affect the outlook of onlookers.

The hospital was full of faces not showing their feelings. The nurses wore their cheeriness like masks. Outside various consulting rooms the parents sat, their smiles fixed stiff, their voices controlled. They were afraid. The children and babies in their arms must be kept ignorant of their fear, the fear of sickness, dying, death. There was a smell of Dettol. Wheelchairs squeaked, trolleys clattered. The ill faces were less sad than the bravery of the parents. Some children wore callipers, heavy plaster casings. The worst expressions were on the mothers who hadn't had their fears confirmed.

'Mrs. Cash and baby Tangerine. You're fortunate that Dr. Greanbach could fit you in.' Kiddies came from all over to consult him. He'd been Uncle Bill to many a sick kiddy. The receptionist took pains with her welcome. A smile made a world of difference to a sick kiddy's Mum and Dad. 'Whoopsadaisy, what a pretty face.'

Dr. Greanbach's waiting room had outsized stuffed animals round the walls. Two lions, a giraffe, a kangaroo, a leather turtle that could be ridden on, looked on with cynical expressions. Ruth's armpits sweated. The receptionist said small kiddies often were the hardiest, not to mention good things in small parcels. Dr. Greanbach was a wonder, what was the trouble did they think?

'She's apathetic, quiet. She doesn't respond.'

Quietness was the kind of illness the receptionist wished more of. A sound she detested was a whining, crying kiddy.

Inside the consulting room were more toys, dolls mostly, arranged in families. Ruth had expected someone fat like Pete to ooze his healing hands over Tangerine. Dr. Greanbach had a wiry neck poking from his overall, a brittle-looking man with overcrowded teeth. He smiled. His overall cracked with starching, the collar framing his neck like the shell of a tortoise. His clothes were loose. He had calm, sad eyes. He waited.

Ruth started gabbling. It was nothing really. The thing of it was she felt anxious. She wanted to make sure, in case of something missed. She was afraid of a mistake.

'Mistake? What do you mean?' He looked again at the letter from her doctor who found nothing wrong. He saw the tense way Ruth held the child.

'Ruth, let the doctor look at her.'

'She seems perfect. A perfect baby.' Easy delivery, no subsequent complications, satisfactory post-natal checks. A beautiful child without a blemish. The mother was the problem.

'What are you afraid of, Mrs. Cash?'

She went on babbling. Nothing, she wasn't afraid. She'd seen the really ill children outside. Tange wasn't deaf or blind. She wasn't plastered, white and dying. She slept a lot. She'd thought it might be a sleep of depression. She realised now how silly that idea was.

He moved adroitly, his hands used to settling children's clothing. He listened, his calm sad eyes watching, his hands testing, alert to malfunction. A beautiful child. Mrs. Cash was on phenobarbitone. Anguished, a classic case of the mother projecting her neurosis onto her child. He heard her out. She repeated that she'd been wrong to be disturbed.

'Disturbance threatens you? Yes? Makes you feel ill? Tired?'

'Perhaps. A bit like that.'

'But growth is disturbance, a disturbance of a kind.' By growing and disturbance you came to terms with life. Sometimes that took courage. Yes?

'She is all right?'

'I can find nothing.' They'd do one or two further tests, routine formality.

In relief, Ruth snapped fasteners, settling wool over her child while the doll family looked on from the shelves. Outside the door the lengthening queue of ill children waited to be touched, made better by Dr. Greanbach, cured while the dolls looked on. The animals and the leather turtle looked at them. By the swing doors was a huge stuffed dog. He explained that a mother could affect her child by her own fears. She was on sedatives, yes? She must forget about aphasia, lorrain's disease, stop consulting medical books. Tangerine showed evidence of high intelligence, was physically perfect. Did she talk and laugh with her? Games, music were important. Did she enjoy her baby? Enjoy caring for her?

Ruth said that Logan did most of it. She'd been too tired, too worried.

He asked if she was resentful. A mother could become so worried that she ended being resentful of the child. Relating started at birth, even before that. Future development lay in the inter-action between baby and parent.

'But I love her, isn't that enough? She's not a mongol, is she?'

'Certainly not. I'd like to know more about you. You're thin. Have you always been as thin?'

'Yes, always. She's not a dwarf?'

'Why should she be a dwarf? You're not tall. Though *you* are above average.' He looked to Logan. Their differing builds were noticeable.

'I should explain that I'm not Tangerine's father. My older brother married Ruth. When he left her I took over. I look after them. We hope to marry when we can.'

'Yes? I understand, yes.' He might have guessed. After thirty years experience he should have sensed something quite unusual. He'd sensed a disconnection. And she was afraid her child was handicapped because of the father's neglect, a retribution, added to which was her own guilt. He asked about her own background. It was unhappy, yes?

'You see I couldn't stand it if she were mad. I dread it. I dread madness. My mother drank.' Madness had made her mother leave. Another kind of madness had made Jordan leave. Would Logan leave her too?

'Yes?'

He listened closely as she described the far-off years. His wiry neck poked further from the starched white. He watched her distress as she spoke about madness, of being sent away, away from Battersea. How, once away, a lady with a garden cared for her. Her gentle foster mother made her happy. Her mad mother came then, took her back to Battersea and madness. Not an unusual story. Mrs. Cash was unusual.

'You see, I want everything perfect.' A safe, perfect life for Tangerine.

'You are afraid of going mad? Yes? You associate motherhood with madness?'

He listened while she described her mother. Her mother lied, cried, fell about. Once she'd soiled her knickers. One Christmas she'd pinned pound notes on the washing line, before demanding more from her father. She described her father, her dread of seeing his face worried. Waiting and worrying about her mother. Her mother's mad face, her father's worried one converged in her mind, she'd wanted to leave both of them.

'You must have hated them. Do you feel bad about hating your mother so?' He wondered what had made her drink. Did Mrs. Cash have any idea?

She spoke about her mother's wartime childhood. When drunk she used to talk about those times, of being evacuated to the country to the house of gentry. Being parted from her mother had affected her. She used to say to Ruth, 'I wish you'd met your Gran. Killed by a V.2. Bombed.'

Dr. Greanbach almost climbed out of his collar. Development of wartime victims, war evacuees fascinated him. Their plight had extraordinary repercussions. He was writing a paper on these cases, about which not enough was known. Here was the actual child and grandchild of one. He asked where the mother was now. He'd like to meet her, meet as many relatives as possible of the fascinating case. Deprived childhood resulting from a neglectful ex-wartime evacuee. There she sat, with husband gone, her brother-in-law stepping in. Already the ginger-headed baby in her arms was marked as scapegoat.

'I don't know. I've no idea.' She was near tears, but less burdened

83

after telling him.

He absently pushed the box of tissues towards her. He was used to patients' tears. She was tensed up. She'd have to learn to absorb her childhood, to let her life develop naturally and freely. Fear and tension were destructive. He asked what Logan did.

Logan explained. First his pride in repairing, restoring damaged articles. Then he spoke of his love of sculpture. He lifted Tangerine from Ruth. He spoke about his plans, how he'd started work on the garden outside his garage. His new, his latest construction would go there, with the other pieces.

Ruth started crying, giving way, bent over by her tears. She rocked back against her chairback, forward against the doctor's desk, a rhythmic rocking. She rocked as mourners or lovers did, abandonedly. She was hysterical. Logan explained that she didn't sleep well. In spite of early bedtimes she tossed, got up to lean over the cradle.

Dr. Greanbach wrote busily. He wanted Ruth to stop all pills. He'd write to her own doctor. He put his pen down, listening again. With calm sad eyes he watched them. The three were what he'd waited for. They'd had their troubles, he had every confidence that they'd win through. Ruth began jabbering about a friend who owned a shop, whose soothsaying had alarmed her, about a friend called Primrose who was jealous, about a cat who'd died. He answered firmly. She must relax. She must talk, sing to her baby. She must take iron, exercise, a sensible diet. She must laugh more. A child echoed the mother's moods. A loving family was the best medicine.

Logan mopped her face. She pushed against the blue hanky ramming her wet face back and forth, a streak of mucus looped from nose to cotton. He tried to hush her, holding Tangerine with his other arm. She wouldn't be assuaged. She was making a time-taking fuss; the doctor had others waiting. Ruth wouldn't stop until she'd finished about the market child, the myrrh, the old doll, the new inflatable one that Logan put into his construction, with the fruit machine.

Dr. Greanbach poured some water for her, sipping some himself without noticing. Witches, buttons, one-armed bandits, it was a surrealist's paradise. And almost lunch-time. Mrs. Cash had her fiancé brother-in-law, whose care was evident, and all three had their health, unlike the many waiting. There were so many with real ills,

84

and not a soul to turn to.

'I'd like to see your work,' he said, opening the door for them. He was interested in modern art. What did Logan make of Paolozzi?

'Logan is outstanding,' Ruth told him quietly, her sobbing ended He made mobiles, large constructions. His work was a worthwhile contribution to art.

He told them to take a holiday, play with Tangerine, be happy. When the swing doors by the large stuffed dog had closed behind them he sipped some more water, wrote more notes before he asked for the next patient. He wondered what the mother, Tangerine's grandmother, was doing.

The receptionist didn't heed Ruth's red eyes. 'There now, little daisy. Got the O.K. then? Thought so.'

'I'll take you to the coast, Ruth.' To Dorset even, if she wanted, he'd do anything, anything to help her.

'Logan, no.' She hitched her shawl up, scrubbing at her cheek with the fringe. Not Dorset, not a holiday. They'd stay at home and finish his construction. They'd go out in the Rolls. She would reorganise, stop being so afraid. Why go near sea water when he hated it? They'd stay in the market, stay at home, finish what was begun. Logan, I will care for you. Lovely times, like Christmas again. We will finish the work to put in the garden.

8

TANGERINE grew. She grew out of her clothes, grew livelier. At ten months she could whistle a carol Ruth had sung to her. The health visitor said that whistling so young was unbelievable. Now the garage was a gay place at night, warm and well-lighted. The construction was almost finished. Logan valued Ruth's opinion. She agreed that the piece had just the ethereal touch he'd intended. Solid as a Rolls he would put perspex sheeting round it, enclosing the figure on three sides. The fourth would be left open for onlookers to walk inside to touch and experience more fully. Sculpture should be lingered over. The perspex semi-transparency would make it more mysterious. The garden would be a perfect background for the strange iron, steel and wooden piece. Rope hair, smelling of linseed, hung from the head of it. Glass parts glistened, the fruit pictures, touched up luminously, were exactly right. He was proud of the quivering hands on the ends of springs protruding from the glass child. The mother's hands were suggested, more like banana bunches with a concrete-roughened finish. Primrose's doll had been a boon after all, part of a lasting work. The child had eyes of juicy lustre like the mother bending to receive it.

'I'm not entirely satisfied. Not bad though' he said, stroking the iron thighbones. It had secrecy. He thought of the time he'd conceived it, sitting above at the kitchen table with Ruth great with child, sorrowing for his brother. Here was the result of their joining, the result of his own joining with Ruth. He shrugged when she said he'd be notable, that critics would acclaim him. Endurance was what counted, application. If one or two spectators liked it he'd be satisfied. An aim was the main concern, a preoccupation with the half-known, following the imagination.

'Would you like to be rich, Logan? Really rich?'

He said that never having quite enough was no bad thing for artists. Money was corrupting. Money would complicate their plain life-style. They owed a debt to Dr. Greanbach. They'd done as Ruth suggested, been to Kew, Ham Common, Richmond Park with picnics packed into the Rolls to eat in green and shady places. Ruth sang a lot. He wanted to get her a violin. She'd spoken of trying to learn, years ago in the country. She was less bitter about that pathetic mother, whose maxim of making good things better wasn't as silly as it sounded. Ruth looked well, her cheeks had a tinge of summer sun. She didn't mope about with dirty toes. She helped. She looked after Tangerine. She helped him in the garden. Together they had cleared the broken masonry. In place of weeds, tin cans, paper and rusty corrugated was green turf. He planned a glass roof extension for more perishable work. His durable pieces were already on the grass. Only 'Fruition' was inside. He'd repointed the garden walls, replacing bricks, and had cemented the open crack. The rats had gone to ground and nasturtiums bloomed in place of the ice-plants. A tangle of orange, yellow, reds, they protruded tongues through the open kitchen window. Ruth said that they were jealous, that their curled petals menaced her. He'd told her any shade of gold or yellow symbolised growth. All the Close garages had once been stables.

With the summer the Doge had cheered up. She liked her lunch hours to stretch into the long warm afternoons. The Cashes were her truest friends. She marvelled at Dr. Greanbach's skill, she wouldn't mind consulting him herself. Ruth was so chipper now, what was his secret? The Cash kitchen was a contrast to her own hot, dark, crowded, smelly one. In Fyste Close she could sit with her mince sandwiches and discuss the world. The Indian had been poorly, though the usual robed figures went filing back and forth out of his alley, the usual piping noises sounded. Mr. Bent, one of the remaining white stall-holders, was starting a sweepstake. He'd been a travelling man in his time, working the P & O lines as cabin steward. He knew Bombay and other eastern parts, knew about money and its slipperiness. He'd told the Doge about the Indian's poorliness and about Mike the street-sweeper's win on Ernie. On such subjects as sweepstakes, ticket lotteries and Bingo the Doge and Mr. Bent saw eye to eye. State-controlled gambling was one of the world's tragedies. The warm weather lost her the few clients she had. In summer they had less cause for complaint. Public holidays were another nuisance. She wondered sometimes if her spirit guides took holidays. Since the brown cat's advent messages came rarely. The cat spat about her spindly calves, banging on purpose to make her spill her oils. The problem of luring clients from public places of amusement was a perennial one. Did you have to have a child to consult Dr. Greanbach?

She scanned Logan's figure, shaking her bun. She walked round slowly, puffing gooseberry smoke over it. 'A clever . . . object, my one.' She admired the way they'd tended the garden, admired it with truthfulness. Though it seemed a pity to put more of his objects out there, cluttering the grass. Privately she thought him wicked to ruin her good fruit-machine. He should have restored it after the young person, his ex flat-mate, had finished spoiling it. Logan had chopped it up, made it grotesque. She could have sold it to an American on Saturday for ten times what Logan had given for it. That's where friendship-selling got you. Now who would want it, all chopped up and stuck into a person's body. That glass baby coming out was quite disgusting, and those springy hands. Enough to frighten her Americans for life. His mobiles had a market, dangling in the breeze and taking little space. No Yank would give a cent for that big thing. Er . . . had Logan thought of having his palm read? Perhaps his karma was at turning point.

Logan went on boring holes in sheets of perspex. With respect he didn't take palmistry seriously. He'd mounted his construction on wooden steps with castors for easy wheeling. Steel uprights would support the perspex. You could ascend them, like entering a shrine, a little solitude with room to walk inside. Not bad, he thought. He said they'd go to Battersea on Saturday.

'Battersea? Why there? Of all places, why there?' Hadn't she told him often enough about it? And of her final leaving, of packing her things in a plastic bag to make for the market, to live there for ever? She hadn't even let herself look at her father's things, his porridge saucepan, his false teeth in the bulb bowl, his presentation watch from his museum. A mild man while alive, his teeth had grinned at her bloodthirstily from the bowl. She'd felt afraid, they'd get her, take revenge on her because she hadn't visited him, had stopped his comforts, fruit juice when he lay dying, needing her, needing his teeth for appearance's sake. She had escaped, had left council employees to deal with his effects, escaped to Jordan and his bookish world. Why go back? Had Logan forgotten her awful life?

'Not where you live. I mean the funfair, the far side of the river. We'll all go in the Rolls. Do you fancy coming, Doge?' Logan had never outgrown the thrill of a fairground. You got ideas in amusement palaces. The brain was activated by danger and excitement when intermingled.

'What, Saturday? No, ta.' The Doge couldn't risk missing her friends from the States. There were fewer that summer, because of the dwindling economy. She must be there behind her till to greet them. They expected her. Would Logan be doing something smaller next? Something more in the line of a mobile she could sell for him?

'My next will be bigger. A sequel to this piece, but larger and heavier.' Probably it would contain a playing child. He'd call it 'Pulse'. He particularly wanted to visit a fairground, teeming with youngsters. Emotional extremes were stimulating.

The Doge sneezed rather wearily. Their garden was a pretty spot. Any news of er . . . Leslie or that little girl?

Ruth had heard Mr. Bent speak about a scrap of a child, running wild in the market, who seemed to belong nowhere. A dangerous thing, a child without its marbles, running loose. Ruth hadn't been curious. Nor was she curious about Leslie. She was learning to appreciate good things. Riding in the Rolls was bliss of a kind she'd not imagined.

For Battersea she put on a salmon-coloured top. Logan had fixed a special seat for Tangerine, her legs poked through the canvas holes like pale grubs. Both of them in salmon, leaning back enjoying it. Like Ruth, Tange didn't tan. She kicked her legs and whistled between bouts of finger-sucking. The people were out enjoying the Indian summer, the streets were thronged. Window-shopping was free. The car attracted notice, the purple emphasising the two redheads, Logan's fair one and their salmon-coloured clothing. Faces looked up from hands fingering knicknacks, blackened silverware, feather boas and sunshades. They envied the happy family in the Rolls. In spite of the de-valuing pound you could be sure of interesting things to look at in the market. Mayfair and Texan drawls mingled with cockney. Late tourists wore creaseproof tartan trousers; their women had pearl chokers with matching earrings. They stared at the strange English currency in their hands before parting with it.

They stared into the Emporium window with its strange mirror behind old things. The Doge kept a bin for old clothes, rags from the Thirties that Londoners liked at that time. The rags brightened the dark step of her entrance, though in spite of them her till bell wasn't tinkling much considering it was Saturday. Ruth saw her wild bun and her grin as they drove past. She had no dollies. She had golliwogs, some lead soldiers, and a china lady whose huge skirts once had covered an old-fashioned telephone. Ruth was able to smile at her fear of dolls. They had no more power now. Logan had put the left-over parts of Primrose's doll under the divan. He'd packed them into the box that had held its clothes, with the price still on it. She could feel appreciation towards Primrose and Pete, still in Cannes, holiday-ing. 'Fruition' owed much to them.

'Drive carefully, Logan.' The robed figures, the Indians, the slitty-eyed Asiatics were indifferent to cars, walking as if they owned the earth, stepping aside for nobody. The Doge's Emporium and the Indian's alley-way were focal points for the Saturday people. Tour-ists found the brown-skinned travellers especially fascinating, star-ing at them. The fascination was not reciprocated by the robed people, who knew they were superior.

'Since when have you worried about my driving?' Logan swerved to avoid a drunk at the top of Church Street. He pitied the weak-spirited. Weakness was something you were born with, you didn't choose it. It worried him to think of Ruth's mother, in want possibly, or worse. He asked what her name was.

'Pearl. Pearl Brown.' She'd heard it shouted often enough. Her mother used to howl at her father. 'Look what you've done to me. I was somebody. When I was Pearl Maggs you thought the world of me. Now I'm Pearl Brown and look at me. That's what marriage to you did.' Ruth felt softer towards her. Logan had done that, had made her more tolerant, forgiving what was done. Brooding, holding griev-ances was senseless. People had the right to choose, to drown sorrows in a bottle or in the ocean. Her mother had once been rather fat. She was exalted to be driven down Church Street in a purple car, owner of a garden, owner of a child with grub-legs kicking. Logan drove beautifully. She'd given the Doge her black cotton shifts for her Saturday bin.

The Bridge was packed with traffic.

'It will be crowded. I love a fair,' he said. He'd choose no other life than that of an artist, sharing with the girl he loved. Ruth, issue of the Browns, owner of Tange, was perfect. The Rolls was perfect. The hot sun made the purple bonnet glisten. On the south side it felt even hotter.

Here the people walked differently, not bargain hunting, window shopping or eyeing each other, but relaxed, their movements slowed down by the heat. Like a weight it dried the throat, the air was thick to breathe. Dirt settled in the crevices of the railings under the parapet. A gull walked the railing, its feathers flattened, aloof from the pigeons pecking at invisible particles of food. There was a smell of petrol. A pleasure steamer passed under them, the pounding engine a beat against the beat of music playing. Couples laughed and danced to the music while steaming up the Thames. He said they mustn't let Tange get sunburnt. He hoped Ruth would like the fair as much as he did. He thought of Tange as his own now, though he looked forward to giving her his own blood child as soon as possible. Tange attracted notice in the market already. Fruiterers put offerings into her pram, oranges, sweet-offerings round her kicking feet, like offerings to a goddess. Sometimes they closed her fists round coins. Mr. Bent put tickets under her pram pillow, having put a suitable entry into his sweepstake book. Logan asked which was Ruth's street, the one where she'd lived.

'Back there somewhere. I don't want to remember it.' Forget the old streets, the mother spoiling that house back there, forget the slummy past, forget the terraced row of houses, peeling paint, the windows hung with dirty net. Forget the dog-messed pavements where it was always stuffy. Winter or summer the street was stale with dirt. A stuffiness that made you sick, a smell you couldn't forget. No greenery or flowers, forget the street that only retained smells, fears, worries. The long hot summers and her mother out late, somewhere, were over. Apprehension set the mould that shaped your later life. Forget, live for today. The only happy times were with the garden lady, she told Logan.

'Didn't you ever go to the fair?' he asked. So near her, the most famous pleasure ground in London, palace of dreams. Soon it was to close down. In hard times even the fair wasn't profiting. A good thing they'd decided to go in time. Today he would make up for what she'd missed, show her what excitement was. The loneliness of a child was the most cruel. Loneliness accounted for her eyes, her lack of friends, her fragile confidence.

'I don't think Tange should go on any rides.' Ruth didn't say she wanted to go home. The heat, the smell of Battersea affected her. She felt sick. She forced a smile, pretended enjoyment for him.

'You don't imagine I'd risk harming her?' He loved every pore of her, would never risk anything stupid. They'd look round only. He might try the rifle range, or shy some coconuts. The fair was the stuff of life, the stuff of creativity. He checked that he had his pencil.

The carpark attendant wore a green eye-shade to protect his face, withered to sultana colour. Sweat and dirt mixed in his wrinkles. Used to a temperature of over ninety he clicked his ticket machine, not speaking. Logan carried Tangerine. He worried about sunstroke. Perhaps they could get her a green eye-shade too. He loved to feel her soft-skinned soles kicking at his arm. Her innocence hadn't a flaw, even her nappies didn't stink like those of other babies. They walked to the roundabout where the toddlers could ride two feet from the ground. Safe within the gaze of their doting parents they circled, wrenching at their steering wheels, proud riders, each one believing themselves in charge. The paintwork, number plates and wheels of each vehicle needed seeing to; it didn't matter. The fair would soon close down. Tangerine whistled her tune.

'No, Logan. She is far too small.'

'Of course she is. I'm not mad, Ruth.' She liked watching. As if he'd leave her for an instant. The small riders fascinated him, their set expressions dazed with illusion of being in control of their destiny. The urge to be self-governing started young. Further in, beyond a turnstile, were the dodgems. The three of them could ride together in a bumping car, no harm could come from that. There was less glare under the roof of the rink, away out of the sun. The neon lights were easier on the eyes. His ideas teemed. It would be like old times. These cars were just the same, the rink was just as noisy as the one in Dorset had been, same noises, same crashes, screams of the riders on their rumbling wheels. His next work might include a pinball machine. It too would be on wheels. These cars were broken too, not worth repairing because of the close-down. These car-poles were eaten brown with rust, their body work was battered. People preferred Bingo to fairgrounds except in sizzling weather.

'She might get jarred.'

'She won't. Not with me in charge. I'll guard you both. Trust me.'
He made her sit close, hang onto his arm, so that his left arm could
encircle them. Here was the heart of it, the noisiest, rowdiest part of
the fair. Here the people screamed loudest. Tangerine pursed her lips,
he couldn't hear if she was whistling or not. The machine-oil smelled
curiously of lemon soda. He picked the least dilapidated car, a red
one. As they were getting into it he caught sight of a familiar leather
jacket. Leslie was boarding a blue car near them. His hair was longer
now. The way his fingers drummed the steering wheel, impatient
to start, was familiar, brought back the past. He hadn't thought about
him for months. He was glad that Ruth was too occupied with Tange
to notice anyone else. Beside Leslie was the market girl. It couldn't be
coincidence, the two must have followed them. The freakish child
was just the same, no older-looking. It was best to ignore them. He
could view Leslie with dispassion now. Leslie had no power left,
pathetic, a nancy in a pretty jacket, failed. A pretty-boy with Asiatic
eyes. He no longer mattered. The damage he'd done in the garage was
long since mended. He could feel Ruth trembling. She mustn't see
the blue car.

'Trust me. Remember that I love you. I will never harm you.' Did
she hear him? He steered from Leslie and the girl in an opposite direction. Forget him. He'd think of the days when Jordan and he had gone
riding in Dorset, old close times when they'd been comrades. Childhood hadn't been all gloom and dead bodies, they'd had happy hours.
Hours spent with their insect collection, afternoons at the funfair.
They used to count the times, who bumped the other most, while
keeping the space between them minimal. Attack, retreat, attack.
Ruth had no need to shake. Leslie was a nobody in a battered blue
car with a mongol clutching at his sleeve, Ruth was his life, he'd let
nothing harm her, nobody would hurt her again. She'd be his wife
one day, and ex-wife of his brother Jordan. How dared Leslie spoil
his work, break into his garage. The cars gathered speed. The increasing speed, the grating of the car-poles against the overhead conductor
was prophetic. His next work would contain parts of cars, wheels,
modes of conveyance.

'Logan . . . please.' She leaned over Tangerine, trying to protect her.

She heard him say that nothing could go wrong while gripping the steering wheel like someone in a trance.

He whirled the wheel to the left. You were controlled by current, the foot pedal and the mercy of the other riders. Who could the market girl be? Odd for Leslie to associate with poverty, ugliness. He sensed their battered blue car approaching from the right, anticipated the crash. A bone-shaking bang. But no harm done. His Ruth was leaning so far over he could only see red hair. It showered, a slippery fall obscuring Tangerine. He thought she moaned. What temerity Leslie had, attacking a mother and child. He'd pay him with his own coin, get him next time round. Ruth must trust, him, remember? Could she hear? Leslie careened again, in front this time, then backing, whoops, missed them. Wrench the wheel round, ready, now, got him in the rear. Again. And there, another from the left, he'd show Leslie, ruining his property, frightening his women. Ruth *was* moaning. Because of Leslie Ruth had got two frights. He could see his face now. Leslie had changed. Corrupt. Lines of corruption showed like Dorian Gray, lines of disintegration. Logan could almost pity him, he had nothing, lacked ambition, was reduced to acts of revenge in the company of a subnormal waif. There was something invincible, enduring about four rolling wheels. He'd do some sketches as soon as they had stopped, preliminary diagrams, shapes. Good Christ, Leslie was trying to demolish them, crashing head-on like a lunatic.

Ruth looked up sideways, hair sticking to her mouth. 'Don't hurt us Logan.' She'd heard of a child getting killed. Had Logan forgotten her fontanelle, with her brain beating against the skin over the gap? She'd do anything, scrub stones, climb mountains, wring bloodied cloths for him, that's what love was, but this riding was too much. You could get broken knee-caps, dislocated backs from bumping cars. They must get off. They must leave Battersea.

'Don't worry, it'll soon be over,' he said. He felt satisfied. That last head-on crash had dislocated Leslie's car-pole. He and the market girl were helpless, would have to wait to be hooked up by the attendant, who would be switching the current off any moment to make all the cars roll to stillness. Strange how a lemon soda smell lingered.

'There, sit up now.' Their ride was over, no more need to bend double or moan over her baby. They had stopped. She hadn't seen the battered blue car, hidden now in a nest of stationary ones in the corner. They were unharmed. He had the theme for 'Pulse' established. Next, paper and pencil. Poor sweet Ruth, humped into her own body like a hairy cocoon, could uncurl herself. Another crowd was waiting at the turnstile to board the bumping cars, ready for ten minutes' thrill, oblivion induced by the risk of splitting their bones to death. He helped Ruth. She was still shaking, her colour was quite gone. But Tangerine was whistling again. The ride had proved that everything between him and Leslie was finished. The spell was dead. He'd catalysed the feelings that he'd hated in himself. He told the fresh onrush of riders to be careful, not to knock Ruth and the baby in their eagerness to board the machines. Odd, the lemon soda smell seemed to have got in Ruth's hair. Leslie and the girl had gone. 'We'll go somewhere quiet now. Sit down and recover.'

There was a peaceful corner, with some trees and grass. The shade cast green-dark shadow, cool to the skin. A kiosk sold ice-cream. Ruth lay back while he fed Tange with small vanilla licks. The big dipper, shots from the rifle range, the roller coaster, the ghost train emitting shrieks could barely be heard here. Ruth rubbed her back. They could forget everything but the green and cool of shady trees. He reached for his pencil. The oak tree dropped caterpillars. They hung suspended by their silk threads. Unripe green acorns scattered over the grass. A grub went down Logan's salmon shirt-neck, two more fell on Ruth's ankle. Soft as the touch of Tangerine's soles, she liked them. She liked the leaves that fluttered coolly above her on the oak tree, liked Logan smoothing her hair back after he'd finished making shapes over his paper. He watched her yellow eyes, her hair over the grass, her cheekbones paled from riding the dangerous cars, her salmon-coloured clothes. He was satisfied with his preliminary 'Pulse' sketches. He told her again that he would always love her, to remember.

'Let's go home.' The Saturday shoppers would have gone, the market would be quiet. The tongues of the orange and yellow nasturtiums would watch them again. They'd drive home, Tangerine still sleeping, put her in the bedroom. The nasturtiums would watch through the kitchen window, the curled tongues wanting a part in the loving and she would feel him, limp first, growing, stiffening before entry, before they moved as one at one with nature, winged insects, free-floating things. Turtles copulated for three days and nights without cease,

95

did he know that? The tongued flowers, herbs in the wall-rack, bulrushes would watch their moving, kissing, loving on the table that had known many things. Brother of Jordan, brother-in-law, true love, lover. Remember that I love you.

'We'll never be able to come again. The fair is closing.'

She said she didn't feel the fascination that he felt for it. That it was sad that he still felt such repugnance for water, sea things. She'd like to go boating, on the Serpentine perhaps, one day.

Near to the carpark was a children's boating pool. Row boats moved over a safe three feet of water. The surface was sheened with floating lolly sticks and paper. Parents could row little children here in peace. Older children manned their own oars. The carpark man sold tickets for half-hour sessions.

Ruth had ridden on the dodgems for his sake, he'd row her on the boating pool. He put the sketches in his pocket, he'd row his loved one and her baby in a small safe boat, while the caterpillars still clung in their hair. Her knees comfortably outspread, she sat opposite him, Tangerine asleep between her feet. She'd steer for him. Here you were quite safe, as safe as Christ on the water, safe in a blue heat-haze while all around them rowlocks squeaked back and forth.

9

'MY ONE, my one, don't look on it as death. Your Logan is in spirit. He's not dead.' The Doge wouldn't wonder if he wasn't trying to get through to Ruth, there in the Ward. He might be trying to communicate that minute. Had Ruth . . . er . . . felt vibrations? She herself had been on tiptoe since the news. Spirits took their own time, you had to wait their pleasure, wait until they'd found a niche on the other side, usually well after the funeral. Wait and be patient. Ruth mustn't look so wretched. A happy release. His earthly body was simply liberated, he'd entered the seven spheres. He was in Summerland. She hoped his messages, when they came, would be more comprehensible than his er . . . object. She wished she'd read his hand in time, though once the mystic influences were resolute it had to happen. Ruth mustn't grieve so. She offered her a sandwich which Ruth refused, not speaking. The Doge was a little hurt. She'd come along for a chat, to hear of possible phenomena, evidence of spiritual communication. Instead Ruth lay as sulky as her own brown mog. Bad little one. And she should eat. How could anyone stay healthy on that hospital diet? She'd brought rations for her, some of her roast rabbits' ears, fern salad, chopped, between bread slices, something to put life into her. Ruth was as white and wretched as a corpse. To die by drowning was a piteous end. And in three feet of water. Britannia might rule the waves; she hadn't safe-guarded that boating pool in Battersea, she'd been out-clevered. The Doge smiled quietly. She said it was well that the place was closing down, a danger to lives and limbs.

Ruth didn't answer. She heard. The deepest grief was what couldn't be shared, you had to get through it. No arms, no shared tears, you had to wait, to swallow medicine, red pills, orange three-cornered ones and yellow. You rested, did what the nurse said and tried to eat. You heard them say it was a pity you couldn't cry. What did it matter if the Doge said Logan was near her? Because he'd died. You thought about him, the feeling of his face, wet, slippery in your hands, the feeling of his hair, your hands remembered and your eyes. You heard the screaming, your own screams and the others. Logan take my sorrow. You heard the splash the boat made as it turned over. You fell. More screams, the others screaming. Hands splashed, the splash of reaching hands, hands in the water. Logan rescued Tangerine, her hair spread like red seaweed, put her in your arms. Take my sorrow. You lost your footing. They came, they splashed their legs through the water, reaching their hands to lift the boat with him under it, face downwards. You saw Leslie and the market girl, you saw their faces. He stayed face downwards, fallen, knocked unconscious. Bear my sorrow. They dragged him out, the screaming helpful people. They said it was too late. Logan I want you. I hear the noise, the shouts, the splashing hands, the dragging. Too late. Logan I need you. I need your face, your warm face kissing mine, your living face, your kisses. They drowned you. That wet, pale, clay-looking thing was your drowned face. I need you, bear my sorrow.

'My poor pale one, your spirit guide will help. You have your own control. Er . . . please take one.' The Doge had her chief magistrate, now Ruth had Logan. She took a calming inhalation of smoke. She had been so fond of Logan. A pity, but it was written, had to be. A pity Ruth didn't fancy her rabbit ear sandwiches. She'd leave her now, go home, re-read the account of it. He had inhaled water. 'Death by asphyxia due to accidental drowning.' There was the picture of Leslie Ackers smiling into the *Daily Mirror* camera, reporting that he and Logan had been good friends. Been with his little sister, who couldn't speak because of her handicap. Their pleasure trip had ended in lament. The Doge read it all most greedily. She did wish Ruth would speak. She hated silence from the living or the dead. A silent person wasn't much better than a silent spirit. Ruth and the sad little sister of Leslie were alike, they couldn't speak. The only silence the Doge tolerated was what she got before a well-attended meeting. Poor Mr. Ackers, no wonder he'd got angry and spoiled Logan's fruit machine, a silent sister with a mental handicap was troubling. This Ward was full of accident cases, too ill to notice her coming or going, or to care what clothes she wore. She hurried out with worried, powdery eyebrows. She'd not expected Ruth to be so low. Without any Cashes Fyste Close was an empty place. Poor pinched, white, child-like corpse. It would be nice if Logan could cure her mog of its spitefulness, before he left Summerland. She would have liked to have kept Tangerine with her.

'Ruth, listen please. Pete and I flew straight back when we heard. We cut our holiday short. Your little girl is safe with us. That old market woman was quite unsuitable to have her. We'll keep her with us in Weybridge till you're up.' Though it was rather inconvenient to say the least. When Primrose had seen the way Tangerine was living in that Emporium she'd had to act. No one could say the Pownde-Wellings didn't stretch a helping hand. It was to be hoped Ruth would recover quickly. The whole affair was typical. Husband gone, boyfriend drowned, no money, job or prospects. Her only other friend a dirty market crone. No gumption, why couldn't she capitalise her assets? Miss Chips mightn't take her now. Why had she re-visited Battersea? The name of it was as repugnant to Primrose as the word grocer. She sent Mrs. Pluto to shop in food halls of large stores rather than pronounce it. Had Ruth been sensible she wouldn't be lying detained for shock, with smelly sandwiches on her locker, looking drowned herself. She'd seen the diary there. Was she still writing nasty things? Buying the costly doll for such a thin-faced tart had been a mistake. She'd found Ruth's child in the crone's kitchen, playing with a leather glove. Primrose had recoiled, but done what she ought, had taken her back to Weybridge.

'I'm truly sorry, Ruth. Time will heal. Pete and I send you our condolences.'

Ruth turned from her. Words from the mouth of Primrose couldn't touch her. Some people couldn't express real truth, they were incapable. Primrose, calling herself friend, extending a plump hand, was false. I hate her eyes, like Leslie's eyes, not true. I saw him, staring at the water, smiling, pushing at the boat with lying eyes. I miss you Logan. They pulled you from the water, gave you the kiss of life, the people shouted, splashed. Gave you a kiss on your clay-looking face. I miss you Logan, miss you, want you, need you. Why aren't you kissing me? The sun shone in your eyes; bright light worried you. Where are you?

'Time heals. I shouldn't bother with a diary. Not just now, it's a trifle morbid.' She didn't trust the tart. She didn't trust her child who wouldn't be parted from its nasty leather glove. Neither showed gratitude. The child spat food about and hit its head. Pete said she was a saint to put up with it. The tart must resume her maternal duties soon.

Ruth looked at her diary. Words, words, words. Consolation, hope. You understand Logan, your work was your determinant. Words are my saving, words on paper, writing words. The right words, putting what I feel. Because you're gone, not with me. I want you Logan, I am lost. I'm suffering a loss.

'Your baby misses you. She says Dada. And did you know she whistles? Of course she has her own room. She does whine rather.' Ruth must understand that the child was sleeping in luxury now, not sharing a windowless cubby hole with the market crone, but in a fine large room alone.

She's not used to sleeping alone. A child shouldn't be left. She will forget you Logan. No father to remember, nor you either. You're gone, she will forget. No sound, no hammering below. 'Pulse' won't be finished. I'm suffering a loss. The pool water smelled rotten. Your eyes were jelly eyes.

'Goodbye Ruth. Try and take an interest in life. You'll soon get over it. I'll kiss the child for you. Goodbye.' Primrose felt like shaking her. Sympathy and pills had made her sulky.

'Ruth, Ruth look at me. Please look. The family told me. They contacted me. They told me about Logan. I've been in Dorset . . . writing.' It wasn't easy, admitting to quarter measure. No Tahiti. Dorset where he'd started. Gauguin's guiding hand had only led him to an old railway carriage near Worth M'Travers. But he'd stuck to his goal, lived on assistance, finished 'Jordan's Banks', put Ruth out of his mind. He never regretted leaving to let his true self take over. He'd had to leave Ruth and the library, leave both to their fate. They were the sacrifice. He couldn't remember parting with her, had blotted the memory out. He remembered leaving the library. Remembered taking tickets, handful by handful, scattering them in trails over the floor, forming a J, its crossbar near the poetry shelf. He'd thrown books in the waste bin, a few more out of the window to make room for his own work when the time came. Ditching them showed his opinion of most current work – a fair comment. He'd gone to the lavatory, swallowed seven glasses of water, returned, inserted his fingers down his throat and vomited, filling the empty ticket recess with a deep and satisfying puddle. For the first time in his life a dirty mess gave him satisfaction. For the first time he'd blessed his delicate stomach. He'd taken care not to splash his beard or jacket lapels, had combed himself afterwards with a quiet mind. Gauguin had seen him through. His colleagues would never laugh at him again. He was to be reckoned with. Feeling gay and purged he'd scribbled a little more with a marking pen on various surfaces, locked up, left for the station, at one with the cosmos. Intending to make for Liverpool, lack of cash had landed him eventually in Dorset once again, Dorset of bitter memory. He'd had to write quickly, because he'd not given up the idea of Tahiti and greenery, was going when he could. In cold and poverty he sat in his converted railway carriage. When the telegram arrived he expected to read of acceptance from the publisher. Instead, it told of Logan's death, signed by his father. Later there was a letter from the publisher. Real heartbreak, they hadn't wanted it. A rejection and a death on the same day. The letter asked him to send postage for the return of his manuscript from London. He'd wept. No book and Logan gone. He'd remembered their fairground sprees, with Logan the bolder of the two, never tiring of riding the bumping cars. Close times when they'd gone insect hunting. Dead now. Why couldn't it have been Ruth or the child? Why Logan? She was alive, thin, red-haired as ever. Her pale silence in the Ward bed was temporary, she'd rise, go on living to do more damage while Logan was gone. How could he ever have called her Ragged Ruth and his own true secretary. Her thin bitch smile was evil. Logan used to wake him gently from nightmares, assist with the killing bottle, inscribing Latin names to the pinned insect bodies.

'Ruth, Ruth listen. The family firm are handling it. Urner wants to know. He wants to know your wishes.' Logan had to be interred fittingly. Since his father had aged his brother Urner ran the business, had sent Jordan to find out. Under Urner's direction the firm still thrived. Cash & Whaler kept their heritage of sympathy, dignity, speed. Ruth had no legal say, he'd come to ask from courtesy. She had no say in anything. Urner had already picked the coffin, hand-carved mahogany, copper-lined and handsome iron embellishments. She wouldn't answer him, unblinking, ashy as a cadaver.

If you shut your eyes Jordan will go away. He's come because he's guilt-ridden, not from caring. He's embarrassed. He's pretending his concern about the burial. I thought I loved him once, how long ago was it? His beard was like Henry VIII once. Damn thing, all straggly now, waggling about graves, waggling about a brother Urner. Come back Logan. Who is Urner? You never spoke of him, are they all mad in Dorset?

'I'll just leave this brochure with you. Urner marked the one he thought you'd like. I'm going back tonight.' He wasn't well. Rejection and death played his stomach up. His position was untenable. Legal husband standing at the bed of his wife who acted as if widowed. Great material was never gathered without suffering. One day he'd write about it, enrich posterity. Meanwhile no one appeared to care that he hadn't enough money for a cup of tea, much less his rent for the converted railway carriage. Urner, issuing instructions, was tight-fisted with the petty funds. He'd tell Urner mahogany, copper-lined, whatever else they wanted. Nobody had approved of Logan in Dorset. Cash & Whaler kept a good face till the end. When adult Logan revolted him, he mourned the childhood escapades in fairgrounds or catching insects, but he wouldn't miss him. Families caused rifts and inconvenience. Gauguin was his family now. The spiritual tie outdid the blood bond. Why didn't those hands pick up the brochure? He'd find another publisher.

What do I care about the straggly bearded fool? He can stick his catalogue. Logan's hands were wetted by the waters, not his. Logan waited while I was in labour. Logan made the home and garden. His warm face, kissing me, where is it? How can I bear it?

'Five minutes then, no more.'
'What only five? What's wrong?'
'Mrs. Cash hasn't been very well.'
'I'm an old friend. Ruth will want to see Mrs. Copper, sick or well.'
'Well Mrs. Copper. Mrs. Cash took aspirin. Not enough to do any real harm. She had some in her sponge bag. She was . . . unwell. She has been distressed about the drowning. Unfortunate.'
'Unfortunate? She tries to kick the bucket with aspirin and you say "unfortunate". Are you human, or are you past caring?' Trust a nig nurse to be hard.

102

'This is a medical ward, not a psychiatric, Mrs. Copper.' They couldn't police the state of every spongebag. In the event the dose had been little more than a gesture. Gestures took up time and skill. They had to use a pump, the patient had become noisy at last, noisy after her silence. She'd moaned like Desdemona as they pushed the tube down. 'Let me go. Just let me go.' A strange girl, isolated. You couldn't predict behaviour, you could only try and rectify. Aspirin and water were the same from any stomach. Mrs. Cash must learn to accept the knocks of life, accept and not evade. She had her baby to look after. Mrs. Copper could see her.

'Ruth? Remember? Remember Mrs. Copper? I never forgot you, never. I saw it in the *Mirror*. Tell me then. The Nurse said you took aspirin. Tell Copper then.'

She'd come at once, in love and sorrow. She'd never forgotten that toothbrush or that doll. What was this aspirin business? Tell her, she would comfort Ruth. Logan was the first and only artist she had met. She'd read about it in her paper, how a Mr. Ackers testified, how Logan lost his footing, bumped his head, too late for saving, how he'd first saved Tangerine. What was this aspirin business?

She kissed Ruth, touched her cheeks with her own tired crying face. They wept together, wept for Logan, wept for Ruth, for everyone. Mrs. Copper said she'd got some money if Ruth needed any, for the expenses.

Ruth wrote to Urner Cash in Dorset. Logan would be buried at her own expense at Golders Green Crematorium. She'd done her mourning. She got up and resumed her life. She fetched Tangerine away from Primrose, took her home.

I O

' "HEART of Jesus, I adore thee. Heart of Mary, I implore thee. Heart of Joseph, pure and just, in these three hearts I place my trust." There now, put your hands together, Tangie, fold them for Pearlie.' If you slept hands folded you could go straight up if your call came. When God wanted you. This was her second chance. She'd not done right by Ruth. She'd come to Fyste Close to make amends. What worried Pearl most was that Tangerine hadn't been baptised. Sleeping with hands folded helped, but if you weren't baptised you went to limbo, you were lost. She'd be a better granny than she'd been a mother. She'd teach Tangie what she'd failed to show Ruth, to make good things better. And she'd teach her devotion. She'd hung a sacred heart over her cot.

'What are you saying to her? Stop it, Pearl.' Ruth stared at her mother. Like a waking nightmare she was back in the house again. Cause of the trouble, the doer of damage had returned. She was a lined-faced travesty with dye-streaked hair whom she couldn't bring herself to call Mother. A pearl was a concretion round a foreign body, this was no pearl, but ugly, an alien person presuming to instruct Tangerine, indoctrinate her with lies.

'I'm only saving her for Jesus, Ruth. Let Granny help.' She'd lapsed herself since childhood. The war and suchlike interfered. She'd started seeing the light again after that poor chap Logan's funeral. She must catch Tangerine in time.

'You're not to interfere. It's lies.' Like a sleuth Pearl sniffed out Mrs. Copper with a brandy-sodden nose. Mrs. Copper had given Pearl her Paddington address at Logan's funeral. Pearl was a nightmare that turned up at funerals. Ruth saw her from the chief mourner's car. The Doge on her right had said 'My one, there is a person waving. Is she known to you?' Mrs. Copper on her left had got out, walked to the swaying figure with the ink-red hair, holding broken stalked flowers, crying easy tears. The past had re-occurred to haunt the nest. She was perverting Tangerine. Mrs. Copper had showed tact, comforting her. Explained how Ruth, bereaved, mourning her brother-in-law, couldn't talk just then, had given Pearl her own address and led her down the street. Pearl read the story in the paper, was in no fit state for a cremation, poor lady, Mrs. Copper understood.

Two years later the doomed woman knocked. With nowhere to go Mrs. Copper took her in, had brought her to Fyste Close. Since the funeral Mrs. Copper had kept in touch with Ruth. She believed in mothers, was pleased to take Pearl to Fyste Close and sanctuary. She took to Pearl. It took one cockney to know another. They didn't pretend. They stayed in their real station, not like Ruth. They'd won no scholarships, they had no arty notions about grammar schools. They knew the fight to get a man, to get his money, the price of fighting for a roof and food. It got more difficult with age. Pearl had nobody. Mrs. Copper's last tiddler, born with Ruth's, had died. She'd lit Pearl's fags for her, whose hands were very shaky, had dried her out for the time being, before taking her to Ruth. Once Pearl got her painful bunions under Ruth's kitchen table, heard that Tangie had no faith, she knew where she belonged.

'It's not lies, Ruth. I'm Catholic. I'm responsible.' Lack of religion had the world in a bad way. Queer immigrants, wogs everywhere, didn't help anyone. She and Mrs. Copper thought alike on that. The market was black with wogs.

'Responsibility? You, responsible?' Ruth saw her mother's weak brown eyes shift. Because of Logan's death she was there, she'd traded on his death. Logan wouldn't turn her away, would let her stay.

'Don't judge, Ruth. I'm here. I want to help now.'

'You call that helping?' When Pearl wasn't sleeping on the divan she was muttering about hearts and adoration over Tangerine. She didn't trust Pearl. She'd been in the home six weeks. Pearl was crafty.

She talked of bettering Tange, said she was a thin pin, odd in her ways, too quiet for almost three. That she should see the doctor where she'd gone before. It had taken two deaths to bring her back to the holy church and her grandkiddy. Ruth told her no more pictures, no holy water, no more praying.

'But Ruth . . .'

'But Ruth nothing. And don't give her a dummy. Damn things. They're bad for children.'

'But Ruth, a kiddy needs love.' It was for Tangie that she'd barely touched a drop since coming to Fyste Close.

Ruth looked at her lumpy feet, the blue veins crawling up her legs, her slippers. Her petticoat had a pinned hem. The roots of her hair were white. Ruth felt no pity. Once Pearl must have captivated her father. Once he'd been beguiled, must once have covered her with kisses, touched her limbs, disrobed that flabby body. Age and drink made bosoms sag. Legs turned veiny. Pearl didn't refer to her past life, had made sure to get her plastic bag of possessions stowed under the divan, where she slept at night. Slippers, the torn petticoat, sponge hair-rollers, a diary for 1960, little else. Mrs. Copper was pleased. Pearl was a nice sort really, if she could control her weakness. When Ruth looked in the diary she saw men's telephone numbers. Prices were listed, varying from three to twenty pounds. She stared closely. Proof that her mother had been a whore, had taken money for it. Pearl was an ex-prostitute. Weekly takings were calculated. When trade lessened, disappeared, she'd gone back to religion. When the body let you down faith compensated. For this, as well as drink, that social worker had stamped 'Recommended fostering.' For this as well as drink Ruth had been labelled 'Withdrawn. An isolated child'. Her mother used to take money and come in drunk too. Correct nomenclature had been ensured early. A child withdrew because of home circumstances. There were many problem homes in Battersea. The home problem recurred at funerals, had followed to Fyste Close. Pearl's religion was charade.

Pearl said that faith was as necessary as money in your purse, bought you a ticket to paradise. Faith got her off the booze, almost leastways, had got the wafer in her mouth in place of the bottle. Let Tangie have the dummy. Ruth had a lovely home. Her old divan was comfy, with room for her things in the plastic bag. She wanted to help. Didn't Ruth believe in anything leastways?

Ruth tried to explain that she and Logan were against anything that didn't allow questioning, exploration. Pearl thought a person must have something. To replace lost loves, empties, lost money. She had Jesus now and the friendship of Mrs. Copper. Sometimes they went to Bingo. What did Ruth mean exactly?

'Freedom to choose.' Logan read Shelley. 'The soul of Adonais like a star, beckons from the abode where the eternal are.' 'Fruition' was still in the garage.

Pearl thought Logan must have been as funny as Ruth. She'd always been unfriendly, not a responsive child. Like her dull father, two of a kind. Both questioned with their eyes, tried to smell her breath to see if she'd had one. They'd driven her away, between the two of them. They made the home so dull. She used to dream of being nice to come home to, like the Cole Porter tune. Once the ring was on her finger things changed. Ruth never had liked her. Distrust went two ways. She never felt the same since she'd come on her in that lady's garden, stripping butterflies to bits. An unfriendly destructive child.

She'd tried to put the home first, but they'd stopped her. You had to please men. Away from Battersea, she'd learned. The war taught her life owed her something different. Evacuated to a family in the country with a governess. The governess showed her and her two sisters gentle ways. She'd not forgotten. Why couldn't Ruth be more like Primrose? Love flew out when criticism looked in. A person had to have something. When your looks went your income went. But Jesus didn't object to bunions, crows' feet, white hair. Anyone would think that Logan was Jesus the way Ruth went on, silly bleeder. A pity she'd missed his funeral. Funerals were something she was fated to be late for, she'd been late for her husband's, who'd been good about sending money, she'd say that for him. She prayed for them, prayed for the dead men. Ruth had some bleeding funny friends. That Doge person made her feel quite funny. A funny kind of palship. Pearl missed her old pub pals. That garden lady where Ruth went was another criticiser. Did it with her eyes. Mouths smiled, said one thing, eyes another. And where was that no-good Ruth had got spliced to? At this rate she'd be on assistance for the rest of her natural, leastways if she didn't buck her ideas up. There was no future in diary-writing, or any kind of writing. It hadn't got the no-good far. Only Primrose had made something of herself. A nice place in Weybridge, another in south France. And no children to spoil it. Tangie was a right thin pin. And such a funny flat, all arty bits and not a sign of Jesus. Jesus understood her bottle under the divan, in case she felt the need. Ruth should have kept Jordan with his steady job. She asked if she still kept diaries. Secretive bleeding pin.

'Just thoughts.' And remembrances. Time was relative. Two weeks, months, years, yet still dead inside, without him. It was a matter of waiting. She would feel whole one day. Pearl didn't help.

Pearl asked why she didn't write some letters. She could understand that. You wrote one and you got one back, leastways you hoped to. Books, diary-writing, was writing into space, you wrote and nothing happened. She used to write letters herself, in her good years, on scented paper, flowery. Clients liked them, liked to remember good times in her company, enjoyment helped by brandy.

'There's no one I want to hear from.'

'No school mates back in Battersea?'

Ruth winced still at the name, avoided saying it. The Doge was loyal. She had become more odd. Her lips were black with smoke and liquorice. Hair and sections of cartilaginous bone from rabbits' ears clung in the folds of her clothing. Business was poor. Pearl said she missed the postman, if only for a bill, a football pool envelope. A card from a car hire service was something.

When the telegram arrived next morning Pearl was agog. Telegrams were rare, still had the power to make her fret.

A reminder of wartime childhood, bad news, parents killed by bombs. They never forecast happiness. Ruth was like her, too sensitive. She'd made a mistake marrying into a funny family. Undertaking was funny work, handling stiffs in a row, waiting to be packaged to Jesus. 'Arriving Wednesday. Urgent – Jordan.' Ruth read it twice.

'Well, what a cheeky bleeder. Mean with the words too.' She'd known it would be bad news, had feared it. What did Ruth make of it? If he came back where would she go? Like weathercocks her bunions twinged. He'd come, another heathen, boot her out. No room at the inn. Sneaky bleeder sending telegrams. Ruth better hadn't see him.

'I'll have to see him. Today is Wednesday.' She'd guessed it in her bones, had known it would be from him. First Pearl, then him. The two who'd harmed her were returning, to harm and haunt a little more, to check her state of being. Soon the bell would ring, ring in his reappearance. She had no choice.

'Ruth, may I come back? I'd like to start again. Can we? Please?' He tried to seem aloof, tried to keep the blush from spreading above the line of his beard. He put his hands in his pockets. He was worn out. She'd changed. He saw her rough hair, the way her fringe grew in her eyes, the way she tensed her hands, not mangling them. She was just as thin. And that was the famous mother, the ogress who had ruined her childhood, standing at the gas cooker, silly-eyed. The wicked mother had lumpen feet and faded hair-roots, was fumbling with the matches, trying to put a light under the kettle. She dropped them one by one, the blackened twists clicking into the bucket under the sink. A smoke trail rose. He hoped it was an augury. He looked at the bare clean kitchen, saw his old divan, saw the corner of the plastic bag under it, guessed it was the wicked mother's bed. Two of a kind, the mother and the daughter moved in with plastic bags when they changed habitat. The mother's trembling hands revived him. He felt less ill.

'You left me Jordan. Remember? You left me when I needed you.'

'I want to start fresh. Begin again.'

'Too much has happened. We can't put the clock back.'

'I know how bitter you must feel. I'll change. I'll be responsible.'

'How dare you come back here. Damn nerve.'

'Please give me a chance. I'll change. I want to.'

'You left me. You left Tangerine. You haven't even asked about her. You left.'

'I'll change.'

'Excuse me, I'm Pearl Brown. I'm here now. I look after Ruth and the little girl. They needed me.' Pearl wouldn't leave without a fight. Her grandkiddy depended on her.

'This is my mother.'

'I'm here Jordan. Ruth needed her old Pearl.' And don't you dare turn me out. My place is here. There, got the bleeding north sea gas lit. Natural mother, natural grandmother. Blood counts. I'm required. Holy water is required in Fyste Close. So go away, you bleeder. Heathen. Tightfist.

'How do you do Mrs. Brown. I have a right, Ruth. I believe I have the right.'

'What right?'

'I didn't want to say. If you insist. I am the owner here. The deeds are in my name. We aren't divorced. I have a right.'

'Why? Why, Jordan? Why now?' She should have known. She might have realised. Remembered the deeds, his legal evidence of right, his just and recognised claim. They were still joined. Her rush to buy the premises had backfired five years later.

'I want you, Ruth. I miss you.'

'I don't believe you. You always were a damn liar.'

'Take no heed, Ruth. He's using you. Leastways, I don't believe it.' Get a word in quick. Before they started bunking up before her very eyes. Tightfisted bleeder.

'I don't understand why, Jordan.'

'I'm lonely Ruth. I need people.' Couldn't she understand? Since Logan's death he'd changed. He felt his situation keenly. He was too isolated. When his writing failed to flower, got stuck in a rut, the thought of Logan going his own way too had comforted him. Logan stood for something. Now there was only himself against an unfriendly world. His family, Cash & Whaler, were against him. Dorset disgusted him. It was too dead. Gauguin wasn't always enough. He'd been served with an eviction notice for arrears of rent. His cold railway carriage was to be taken from him, but posterity mustn't suffer. He'd go back and write his books, ensure they stood on library shelves. He thought of Logan working patiently in the garage. It had a tap and stove, was warm and weatherproof. He missed him frightfully, wept for the lost boyhood companion, brother in creative work. He was entitled to it. Fyste Close was central. He'd noticed the social decline of the market when he arrived, all blacks and broken windows, smells. No matter, he would stay. He didn't insist yet on the renewal of marriage rights. He'd find an agent first, be on the spot, ready to sign a limited number of copies, attend press parties when the time came.

'No, Jordan.'

'I'm the owner. I only ask to live below. I have legal and moral entrance. I shall use the garage.'

'No Ruth. He wants a woman, that's his game, a woman.' Bleeder.

I I

THE winter was a mild one. The leaves uncurled again, a green mist in the light spring mornings. Instead of hammering there came tapping from below. Jordan took the typewriter from under the divan. He wouldn't ask for her secretarial help yet, she'd let him down before, had been treacherous. He pecked out words with two fingers, cursing.

Ruth's heart felt deformed, as if it would never recover. No. 3 had witnessed various sounds, the scratch of mice, the rattling glasses on the table under her and Jordan, iceplant stalks, leaves over frosted cobblestones. The rub of the garage door over the hardpacked snow, Tangerine's quiet noises. Angel chimes, the cat that growled and tore at the old doll. The sound she heard most often now was the light slow tap of Jordan typing. Her heart felt twisted.

Jordan was all right. Exalted, he could go to work. He'd won. Free quarters, a warm workplace. He'd make No. 3 famous. He saw the commemorative blue plaque over the door in his mind's eye. They'd come for miles to see it in fifty years time. When he wasn't tapping he spent time pondering through the window overlooking the garden and Logan's queer sculpture. 'Jordan's Banks' had been refused by many agents. Cards kept coming requesting him to collect his manuscript. He went on doggedly, seeking a firm of sufficient perception. He wouldn't dream of cutting a word of his hundred and twenty thousand, he didn't believe in re-writing. His volume would grace coffee tables throughout the world, printed on India paper. Only a quality publishing house could undertake such a costly production at a time of inflation. He could afford to wait for acclaim. He only asked for peace and as little contact as possible with the family upstairs. Especially the daughter. He avoided looking at her. He disliked all children, particularly girls. They bored him to the point of nausea, a nausea that often included the whole human race. The small waif-thin girl (he never thought of her as 'his') had the same long, saddened eyes as Ruth. Her hair and odd ways made him uncomfortable. For the sake of his writing he forced himself to ignore her existence. Luckily they both kept quiet. Pearl was the noisy one.

He'd made short work of Logan's things, his car, his bench and tools, his lathe, drill, spray compressor, his substantial vice, all gone to the Doge except for his statue contrivance. Ruth wouldn't let him touch that – a condition of his re-admittance, he mustn't touch it. It was impossibly heavy. Like a relic, she'd wrapped an old green eiderdown around it. The thing made him as uncomfortable as the child did. He'd lost interest in Logan now. He had the garage. Child-hood times, rides, insect chasing, over. Thanks to Logan he had a fine north light. The garden would be nice in the summer months, but for the queer sculpture. With his national assistance organised locally his conscience was immaculate. It made him feel noble to give a pound or two to Pearl, to give to Ruth who'd only married him for an easy life. She'd not honoured her promise to type for him. Let her stay above, the slatternly mother bitch who'd thrown away his furniture. Down-stairs was all right. He got used to Pearl, a harmless creature who sang a lot. With the addition of a bed, a carpet and other items the garage was a vast improvement on the Dorset railway carriage. He'd start another book.

'Look, Jordan, seeing as I'm legally your ma-in-law you might as well drink this.' Pearl had found a matching mug and saucer. She'd got a nice tin tray from soap coupons, was introducing small changes without Ruth noticing. Upstairs was so dull and bare. No harm to pal with Jordan, undertaker though he once was, no harm in palship leastways.

'I'll drink with gratitude and pleasure, Mrs. Brown.' How one gene-ration differed from another. Ruth, issue of the Browns, was another species. He sipped. He'd learned the value of manners and punctilio from his father and the public library. Well-chosen remarks, sincer-ity, could make the difference between a full or empty stomach, a good roof or a leaking shed in Dorset. Manners could line or blow away the nest. She asked him to call her Pearl. It was a happy cup of tea. With narrowed eyes she didn't look quite so repellent. In no time she'd be putting Osborne biscuits in his saucer. He remembered his father tell-ing him never to ignore a boring or inferior person. Everybody died. All creatures made a corpse, were worth a smile and thank you.

So when Primrose stepped from her yellow Citroen one morning he walked over the cobbles to her with his umbrella. 'Let me shelter you. Don't let those sweet curls get wet.' She was worth a minute of his writing time. Since Pearl and he had fraternised his shirts got ironed, his socks seen to. He'd like a word before Primrose went up. Had Ruth told her he'd returned?

'She did. She told me on the telephone. You can scarcely expect me to applaud, can you?' Jordan actually sounded cocky, as if expecting admiration.

'I expect nothing, Primrose, except a chance to prove myself. A second chance.' He looked into her eyes unblinkingly, putting his soul into his own. With more allegiance his work would prosper.

Primrose said that she and Pete regretted the whole affair. Their fears for Ruth's marriage were rather justified, weren't they?

'I know. I know.' He lowered his lids in humility. How fortunate that he'd kept his librarian's suit. Primrose was always in fur and angora, a plate-glass window. No rags or hippy sandals on *her* body. He added that he was just a tenant, in a way of speaking. He told her how pleased he was that Ruth had her mother, Pearl, upstairs. Primrose must understand how changed and serious he was. Ruth needed her mother. Mother and daughter had been through tough times. He was in part to blame, admittedly. Meanwhile he was there, downstairs if he was needed. He hoped to reinstate himself one day. He begged Primrose to step into his garage, just for a moment, out of the rain. He told her that Ruth relied on her friendship, he'd like Primrose to feel she could rely on him. His voice throbbed, tears almost touched the corners of his eyes. The strength of his sincerity quite drained him. He raised his hand; his beard was perfect. Buckingham Palace wouldn't turn him away. Please.

'All right. Just for a moment. Writing, Jordan? Still?' She was rather short-sighted. She peered at the paper by the typewriter. He offered her a sheet. Two publishers were interested, he explained. She looked at the white sheet with distended blue eyes. She could see nothing. He explained that he was waiting for the highest offer. He wanted to make as much money as possible to give to Ruth. He'd show their letters to him, only they were with his agent. Able chap, keen to act on his behalf. Primrose must believe that his present intention towards Ruth was honourable, responsible. Here, read a page or two more. He heaped the stapled chapters into her large hands.

'Two publishers? Really? I had no idea. That's rather wonderful, Jordan.' It showed how one could be mistaken. He was no charlatan, she'd been wrong to write him off as a bad buy on Ruth's part. Typical of the thin-faced tart to say nothing of his success on the telephone. She listened closely as he told her more. How he'd been offered a job as Features editor on the *Observer*. Of course he'd turned that down, his writing came first absolutely.

'Of course. You had to,' Primrose murmured. Features editor. She couldn't wait to tell Pete. All wasted on that tart upstairs. He explained the necessity of a well-presented book. He'd settle for the chap who thought as he did, was prepared to spend most on production and promotion. Presentation mattered. Appearance was essential in the world of art. He foresaw the moneyed fingers lifting his opus from a morocco box container, the picture made him quiver. He already believed the story about the *Observer*, two publishers and the agent.

'I do so agree,' said Primrose. A genius. How could she have maligned him? She'd never read much. That must change. She'd get some glasses, see every word he'd done. She wished she'd been more intellectually inclined, instead of sticking to the captions under the the pictures in Mrs. Pluto's 'Titbits' in the kitchen, or re-reading her notes to her employees, delighting in her skill. She wanted to help Jordan. The thin-faced tart was no assistance, hindrance rather. She didn't even type for him, when two publishers were waiting. She'd rather grieve for her greaser. Jordan was too good to earn money in the usual way, too good for anything mundane. Primrose turned her back on the thing under the green eiderdown. Ignore any trace of the greaser. Jordan, returned, was a man of strength and character.

'I worry about Ruth and my . . . family. I may have to return to the library, the cost of living being what it is.' He looked closely into her popping eyes. A family was a big expense.

To his delight he heard her say he mustn't think of that. She'd be proud and happy to subsidise him until his royalties started rolling in. Nobody need know. She appreciated his reluctance, but she'd look on it as a privilege. She'd be his protectress. He must carry on until he heard from his agent which publisher would be the wisest choice. Their secret. Meanwhile, could she help? Make notes? File things?

Look up some words? Not that he'd ever be stuck for one of course, but small things. Paper? Stamps? She blessed him for stepping out with his umbrella. 'Growth in the Green', 'No More' were the best titles she'd ever heard. The world looked new. A writer needed her. She would contact her bank manager, he could depend on her.

'Well, Prim, long time no see.' Pearl eased her sore toes. She missed someone to parley with. Mrs. Copper was having trouble with Old Copper, hadn't been over recently. She used to dislike Primrose as a child who'd been another criticiser. But she'd encouraged Ruth to go to Primrose's home, to eat fries and grocer's cake and save her the bother. She'd make up now, leastways she'd try to. Some spag on toast, mashed spuds and Osbornes spread with jam would be a change from Weybridge fare. It went to show weight didn't matter. As fat as ever yet she had a lovely home. Pearl wished Prim was her daughter. Prim had made something of life. Ruth was a moper who made no effort to get another man and didn't like her cooking. Peter Pownde-Welling was interested in the stock market so Pearl understood. She knew a little about giving comfort with the hands herself. Comfort and a well-filled sock could change life's face, leastways make a lot of difference. It pleased Pearl that Jordan liked her food. She carried covered trays down regularly. It pleased her to be needed. She'd christen Tange if she had to do it with brandy. Thin pin, nobody's child. Pearl worried in case she was soft-headed.

'How are you, Mrs. . . . . Brown?' Had Ruth's mother re-married or not? She didn't remember her. Ruth was the only remnant of Battersea that survived. She saw now why. Remembering, keeping contact with Ruth had led to Jordan.

'Pearl to you, Prim. Pearl to my friends. I'm still Ruthie's Mum, though you might be excused if you forgot. I'm seeing to things here.' She lowered her voice, glancing in the direction of the bedroom where Ruth and Tangerine were. They had a habit of shutting themselves away, suspicious little bleeders, both of them. But she worried about them.

Primrose stared. She remembered Ruth's accounts of life at home. Here was the mother who ran off and left her, returning after poverty and brandy had taken any looks away. She looked fleshless, her back bent into a bony 'S' shape. Those flabby loins had produced a daughter who had married genius. For that, she deserved respect.

Primrose extended a hogskinned hand, showed a gold back-tooth in a smile at Pearl. They got chatting. They agreed that Jordan had surprised them, he'd not received the respect he deserved. Soon they were sitting at a table agreeing over Jordan, agreeing that Logan's kind of art was boring, agreeing about I.T.V. commercials, 'Miss World', that Britain should be kept white. They agreed it was surprising that they both got on. Jordan had brought them together. Women were the same under the skin, if you found a common liking. They'd both help Jordan to fame.

With his two new accomplices Jordan set his goal at a minimum of a hundred words a day. He finished re-numbering the pages of 'By Jordan's Banks'. He believed that what he'd forecast would come true, but often it was so pleasant to have Pearl and Primrose with him that he only managed five words. Primrose came each morning. They gave him comfort, praise and snacks of battered fish, with doorstep sandwiches made by Pearl. Jordan put on weight, and Primrose's clean extremities puffed larger. Days of writing nothing at all were justified by the knowledge that he was gathering material. The women were good copy and they listened. They heard again and again about the two publishers, the *Observer* begging him to join their staff, letters all kept by his agent. These tangles took time to unknot, he told them. His imagination rioted. He told about his time as a foreign correspondent in Yugoslavia. He managed to stop himself from saying that he'd won the Nobel under a pseudonym. He told them about Gauguin. Neither had heard of him, though Primrose nodded sagely. It was all compensation for the loneliness of Dorset. He said nothing of his family, how they'd sneered. How Urner wouldn't speak to him. He might as well be dead as far as Dorset was concerned. Pearl read hesitantly, Primrose found it a strain, but they had ears. They were great company during those long rainy mornings. It rained persistently, heavy sheeting rain, running down the panes, a watery insulation against the cruel world outside. The only sour note in their haven was that thing under the green eiderdown. They sat with their backs to it.

One morning they heard a heavy soaked tread outside on the cobbles. Rain ran down the broken spines of Mrs. Copper's umbrella. Her nose was pink. It glistened wetly under a small tear in the black cotton. It was pink too from Old Copper's temper. She'd missed visiting. Old Copper let out at her in his rages, but she was better now. She'd heard talking, had tapped on the garage door before going up to Ruth. She loved a party. So the three became a foursome, dividing quickly into two camps. Pearl and Mrs. Copper discussed Bingo and their fancies for the White City dog races while Jordan read sections of 'Growth in the Green' to Primrose in a throbbing voice. The buzz of sounds rose through the floorboards to Ruth and Tangerine upstairs. Pearl couldn't wait to get down there each morning. It was so dead upstairs, she told her cockney companion as she took Mrs. Copper's headscarf from her, spreading it before the electric fire. She left her umbrella opened in front of the eiderdowned figure, to help conceal a little bit of it. Jordan was happy to have Primrose to himself. Astonishing that he'd not recognised her value in the old days. Her beauty was as abundant as her admiration. 'Brilliant', she whispered, at the turn of every page, and gobbled Osborne biscuits spread with jam.

'Marvellous really, what a writer can do when he tries', said Mrs. Copper, feeling her nose to see if it still hurt, mopping herself with her scarf. The rain continued for weeks. She told Pearl that Old Copper was specially interested in that drowning, she'd told him about meeting Logan in hospital. It made the story in the paper so real. He was interested in the real true husband back now in his place, taking over again from the drowned brother two years later. A writer was a handy thing, stocked libraries for educated people to spend time in. A shame he had to put up with those nigs in the market place, breeding like animals about the place, no fit companions for a tiddler of Ruth's. She was all for Jordan. Not that Logan hadn't been a winner. Some sculpture was difficult to understand, the kind like those bits in the garden, getting all wet now.

Ruth went on keeping her diary. The daily space wasn't large enough; she overflowed onto sheets of foolscap. She didn't mind solitude if she had paper and her sharpened pencils. There was so little now to show that Logan had lived there. The garden outside was a memorial, with the rain running off the iron sculpture. When grief abated, a fallow time set in, a time of trying to find balance. To survive you must adjust. She must try and trust Jordan, legal husband who had rights. He paid her an occasional pound, she couldn't stop him believing he had a contribution to society in his books. She

117

must try and trust Pearl, who scrubbed the floors clean and didn't crave her brandy much, now she had Mrs. Copper and Jordan to visit each day. She must try and have faith in a future without Logan, live for Tangerine who was too quiet. Tangerine rarely spoke, a glass-encased child who stared and had odd mannerisms. At nearly three she should be speaking fluently. She wrote about these worries. She wrote everything she could remember about Logan. She'd never love like that again. She'd like 'Fruition' in the kitchen, a reminder.

'What's that big thing, Ruth? I live here too. I couldn't stand it. Leastways not in the kitchen where I sleep.'

'I would with pleasure, Ruth. It takes up too much space. But it's so heavy, how could I carry it upstairs? The floor mightn't stand up to it.' Jordan would be more than glad to be rid of it. Already he was planning the arrangement of the garage when he was dead and gone. His home, open to the public, the blue plaque outside the study doors. He insisted that the word 'garage' was dropped from the vocabulary of Primrose, Pearl and Mrs. Copper, referred often to 'my study'. He blamed the statue sometimes for his lack of creative flow. His three women helped counteract its menacing presence. But for Ruth and it being so toughly built he'd demolish it with a sledge-hammer.

'Cheer up, Ruth. No sense looking back. You have to live for now.' Life was a bleeder all right. Pearl was saving Green Shield stamps to get a toy for Tangerine. More like a crab than a butterfly, you wound it up to make it flap its metal wings and scuttle. Had Ruth seen how slow Tangie was? At that age she should be playing. She had no toys, leastways only that nasty glove of Logan's. How about a priest, had Ruth considered getting in touch with one?

'I agree with Pearl. The child looks a trifle odd,' said Primrose, though she had no interest in the child. Jordan's work besotted her, nothing upstairs was her concern now, only Jordan and his writing. She saw now what an expensive time-consuming nuisance a child was. She'd peered under the green eiderdown to see what kind of a monstrosity the greaser had made. She'd seen the parts of her expensive doll, parts of it broken up, stuck into the endeavour of a lunatic. Logan must have been as loco as Ruth. It wasn't surprising if the child was wanting. He'd stolen a child's toy for his mad purpose, broken it and died. She felt washed with sympathy for Jordan,

involved with two psychopaths. Where was the rest of her doll?
Where had the madman put it? The thin-faced tart and her child
should see a specialist. After looking under the green eiderdown
she'd had to make a real effort to listen to Jordan reading his wonderful book. She practised her expression of facial understanding before her mirror in Weybridge, wetting her lips fetchingly. She hated
Ruth's smell. Pete was doing unusually well in private investments.
She'd get an electric typewriter for Jordan.

12

'OF COURSE. I do remember you, Mrs. Cash. You came once only. I remember Tangerine. I remember . . . your . . . brother-in-law. When we saw no more of you we assumed that all was well. Yes?' The child alerted Dr. Greanbach's attention. He noticed instantly her lack of sociable reaction. She showed no curiosity, nor was she uneasy. She didn't look to her mother for reassurance. He wondered if Mrs. Cash had married since. He watched the child fingering an old glove, apathetically. She was cut off.

'Logan died.' Ruth spoke flatly.

'I . . . I am sorry. Really sorry. He seemed to me to be . . . outstanding. How very sad.' Mrs. Cash seemed as indifferent, flat in her manner as the child. He never got used to the finality of death, the particular helplessness induced by it. Finished, checkmate. Ill-health was his livelihood. Ill people kept him going. Sad. He asked her to tell him about it.

'It happened ages ago, when Tange was seven months.'

The hospital was the same, the leather turtle, the lions with cynical expressions, the giraffe and the dog. The mothers waited like a tableau, guarding their children in callipers and heavy plaster casings. They wore their pinned-on smiles, the same receptionist led them to the inner waiting room where the same dolls stared. Only Ruth felt old now. The meaning of her life was gone. Logan was gone. He'd drowned.

'Drowned, did you say?' He noticed Tangerine dropped the glove, moving her hands like fins. She pursed her lips in a whistling movement. He asked to be told more, that is, if she would.

'No.' The past was over. Ruth saw his wiry neck poke from the shell-stiffness of his overall, his crowded smiling teeth, his calm sad watchful eyes. But Logan wasn't there to mop her tears or to control her babbling. He'd got drowned. Life over. It had taken all her strength to get to the hospital. Tangerine had refused to walk. Too big to be carried, people stared. Mother and daughter, dead-eyed, indifferent, tired. Her arms ached. She felt wrecked.

'He was an artist, I remember.' He remembered his self-sacrificing love. He'd like to have seen more of the family, had hoped for an answer to his follow-up enquiry, had been disappointed. At the time he'd been writing a paper on the descendants of war evacuees. How was her war-scarred mother? Still alive? Er . . . she had a drink problem, he remembered. He watched Tangerine's pursed lips, her fishlike movements.

'She's living with us. In the market. She wanted me to come. She thinks Tange is soft in the head.'

Mrs. Copper had taken up the cry as well. Ruth must return to the clever man who'd helped her once before. Tange hardly knew her own name.

'Tell me about it, Mrs. Cash. You look tired. Sit back. Come Tangerine, show me that pretty dress.' Adult trauma could push a child into withdrawal, a privacy, sealed, hard as diamond. He spoke again to her. She didn't look at him. She heard the sounds coming from his toothy mouth, heard a smile in his voice. You didn't have to notice. Gurgle sounds. Like being in your bath you heard a gurgling when you put your head back. Sounds didn't matter. You felt wet in your hair, warm, nice, you didn't care. You could pretend not to hear things. 'I Saw Three Ships Go Sailing, Sailing by.'

'Tangerine, let me show you. What is this?' He picked the glove up. An old glove, gauntleted, for motoring, its surface peeled in patches, as though marked by teeth. He saw her unfocused eyes, the set of her mouth. She knew what he was holding, he sensed cognition.

He is holding something. You know what. Don't look. You don't have to. You do not have to walk or talk if you don't want. You don't have to hear the toothy mouth or look at what he's holding. 'Three Pretty Maids Were In them, In them'. Warm water is quite safe, nice. Do not look.

'Tangerine. Disgusting girl. What are you thinking of? She's always clean at home. She has been for years. Whatever's wrong with her?'

'Don't worry, Mrs. Cash. We're used to small accidents here. Large ones too. She's a little nervous. Come Tangerine, come over here.'

You don't have to move. You can sit still on your chair, that you've made warm and wet. You can whistle, you don't have to listen any more.

Dr. Greanbach gestured to the sink in the corner. Many mothers had strong views on the subject of training. A dirty child was a mark of failure. Mrs. Cash was mopping the floor as if she'd been caught sinning, rinsing the child's legs frantically.

'I'm sorry.' Water had heralded her birth, water had killed Logan, water was disgracing her in Dr. Greanbach's consulting room. Pearl wanted to splash more of it over her for baptismal purposes when she wasn't washing floors. The body was ninety per cent water. To think about it was enervating. Ruth wished she lived in a field, without plumbing or hygienic standards, only peace.

Dr. Greanbach didn't move away, went on holding the glove to Tangerine. 'You like this? Take it, won't you?'

He's holding the glove. You needn't look. Your Mum is cross about the water. Don't listen to them, making their noises, worrying. Grown-up people cry and worry. 'One Could Whistle, And One Could Sing, One Could Play The Violin'.

He wrote notes, looked up the file again. Had she always whistled so clearly?

'She whistles and she waves her hands. She has for ages.' Pearl and Mrs. Copper found her an entertaining sight, agreeing that she was unnatural.

He was surprised, in view of her disquiet, that she'd not sought advice earlier. Hadn't the Health Visitor called?

'Someone called. Someone left notes.' She never answered the door, but lay on her mattress every morning listening to the buzz of Jordan and his female reinforcements down below. Tangerine waved her hands in her sleep sometimes. Upstairs the time passed blankly.

Dr. Greanbach looked at her eyes under a special lamp. She didn't appear to notice, continuing to wave her hands. With the beam of light in her pupils she started nodding, puppet-headed motions, her hair, long like Ruth's now, flip-flapping. Suddenly she screwed her head and bit his hand. He didn't start, his eyes stayed calm and watchful. Blood showed from the line of her toothmarks, pinheads gathering into drops. He blotted them, throwing the reddened Klee-

122

nex into the bin. It was important not to react. You got used to the unexpected. Incontinence and violence were symptoms of fear. He told
the mother to stay calm, not to worry.

'What is it? What is wrong with her?' Not content with wetting
she'd bitten his helping hand, wrapped now in another Kleenex.
Water, blood, what would she do next, what limits would she go
to? Ruth felt like hitting Tangerine. Her dress smelled. What a beast
she was. Her socks had brown patches where the dress dye ran.
And she looked silly, wagging, waving without sense. What was
wrong?

'I'd like to ask you a few questions, Mrs. Cash.' About her eating,
sleeping habits. Did Tangerine dress herself? Who did she play
with, and what games? He went on stroking her hair rhythmically,
disregarding her lack of reaction. She went on whistling the same
tune, blank-faced.

'She's solitary. We both are, I suppose.' She played in the garden.
In the afternoons, not ordinary playing, running to and fro, spinning
tiptoed, without purpose. Sometimes she tapped the sculpture absently. She never came when called, or noticed different faces. You
would expect a child to know her own mother. Ruth said there
were no other children. The Close was a cul-de-sac, the other buildings tumbled down or used for storage, were rented by the market
people who were mostly black now. Not that it mattered. Tangerine
wouldn't notice another child. She didn't notice the women below.
Nothing mattered. Pearl dressed and fed Tangerine.

'No toys? No special plaything?'

'The glove.' Logan's old one. She rocked it sometimes, waved it,
running in the garden without purpose.

He asked Ruth if she ever tried to play, occupy Tangerine's attention, read to her.

'The thing of it is, I'm always tired.' She didn't blame Tange for
preferring a mad land, more pleasing to her than a mother who
couldn't be bothered and was sad. A child needed fun. She'd even
thought of offering her to Mrs. Copper who understood a tiddler's
needs. She had already given her the electric toothbrush, Logan's
gift. In Paddington they'd all take turns at it, Mrs. Copper polishing
her few weak ones, the tiddlers whitened their blackened teeth,
rectifying the damage of unwise sugar intake. Mrs. Copper had been

lyrical, pink nose shining. Adults had a remedy at hand, could turn from the pain of reality to aspirin, drink, bingo or a mechanical device. Tange waved her hands as her alternative. The three women were besotted by Jordan and his work.

'Do you hear me, Mrs. Cash? You understand me?'

'What?'

'I'm saying to you that I think Tangerine should come in. For observation.'

'Why?'

'She needs tests. Special care and notice. We need her for a while, until we know for certain. You understand me, yes?'

'Don't take her. Things will get better.'

'Just for a while, a little while.' He sighed. Maladies that affected the whole family were saddest, the most difficult. He made himself smile. Patients must go on trusting him, as he must trust in himself, his skill. Inadequacy must never crack the surface of professionalism.

'You won't keep her?'

'No, no. But you need rest. You look worn out. The present situation isn't viable for either of you.'

'What's wrong with her? Don't take her. I'll improve. I'll play, I'll read, I'll take her out. I need her.'

'She needs you, Mrs. Cash, make no mistake. You want her better? Yes?'

'What's wrong? She wetted. She bit you. But why do you want to take her?'

He explained that tests were vital. It could be a variety of causes, a vitamin deficiency, an allergy to diet, a number of reasons.

'A friend gave me some tablets.' She had given Tange some. A recent sideline of the Doge was tablets made from poppies, for those low in spirit. The time went quicker when you ate them, you slept longer. 'Made from fresh petals. Administer sparingly for the under tens', the Indian had printed under a poppy decoration.

Dr. Greanbach asked to see the bottle, remembering how she'd babbled about sorcery, a friend in the market who sold dolls and concoctions when she'd come before. Obviously she was easily swayed. A tragedy to lose her brother-in-law who'd provided much-needed emotional ballast. She should never touch anything unprescribed. Had she other friends?

124

'The Doge is my real friend. Since Jordan came back. He's my husband, Tange's father. We never got divorced. He lives below the flat in the garage. He . . . writes. I rely on the Doge.' The Doge worried about her, brought her myrrh, roast rabbits' ears in dark times, comforted her with pills. The Doge said Tange's whistling was significant, a sign she'd be a medium. Child mediums, poor little brats, were not like others. Hand-waving could be another sign. She advised Ruth not to go back to the good doctor, but to trust her poppy pills. Advised her to have no dealings with the garage lot. Unhealthy persons, all. Those women shouldn't be there. That's what newspaper reading had done. Because of reading papers three unnecessary women had collected in Fyste Close. Pearl was worst, sleeping in Ruth's kitchen. Weak woman and her bottle who had turned to Jesus. The Doge had nothing against Jesus, only attendance at her meetings was better, would do more good. She'd never had any opinion of Mrs. Copper, credulous soul who would believe any-thing. Primrose had snatched the brat from her care when Ruth was in hospital after the tragedy, she couldn't forgive that. She knew little about the father of Tangerine.

'No one else?'

Ruth told him about Primrose, how they'd been friends at school, how their lives diverged since. How Primrose had no child. Primrose would be glad if Tange were diagnosed a gremlin. Mrs. Copper would be sorry, but tiddlers were prone to ailments. Jordan had never spoken to her.

'He lives below and she has no contact with him. None at all?'

'He lives there, I told you. We don't meet.' What was wrong? What did Tange have?

He said she showed signs of autism. There were indications. Too early to be definite without further examining. She showed classic characteristics; indifference to surroundings, a failure to relate, un-due absorption over one object or total unconcern. Irrational biting, arm waving. He was interested in her description of her spinning, running with no purpose in the garden. The family relationships were unusually sundered. Her whistling like that was most unusual. Mrs. Cash would hear as soon as there was a bed vacant.

'Could you take her if she went privately?' She could ask the garage lot to contribute. Tange was an embarrassment to them, out there in the garden acting strangely. But if she was taken from her she'd have no one. No one to answer for, no one of her own. It was important to be needed. It was important to need someone.

'I don't work privately, Mrs. Cash. Each patient is treated equally by me. You'll hear from us as soon as possible.' He wished he had more faith in her ability to meet trouble. He made a note that the social worker must maintain contact. She looked half alive, needed sustained visiting. He'd been proud of his 'Victim' paper, he could look forward next to an opportunity of hearing about the war-scarred mother of Mrs. Cash, and the deceased brother-in-law's sculpture. What had happened to it?

Ruth told him that she'd been approached by a dealer in Mayfair. He wanted examples of recent sculpture, had been impressed by 'Fruition' and the other garden pieces.

Jordan's eyes went into a state of hatred when the eiderdown was removed. Dr. Greanbach said she should stop all herbal remedies, there were more modern ways of dealing with depression. Her husband wrote? Talent in the family, obviously. Was her mother gifted, a singer perhaps, an actress, yes? Which did Mrs. Cash favour, which creative bent?

Ruth shook her head indifferently. Her diaries were important to her, not worth telling about. Jordan, poseur, cut-off in Dorset like a dog, the result of a screwy upbringing in Dorset, was no writer. Her mother, source of shame, illiterate ex-whore, was no actress. Logan, with his work beginning to flower, was dead. Mrs. Copper had a heart, had been a wholesome friend, but changed since knowing Jordan. Must Tange go? He showed his overcrowded teeth again, nodding. Leave it to him.

The Doge cried out. 'My one autistic? I've heard a lot about it. Poppy pills. Her mystic influences are revealing.' She sneezed three times.

'Dr. Greanbach said no. No pills.'

'Autisticness goes with overstrain. Those pills would help.' Ruth needed her. Since Jordan came back, he and his followers had spoiled Fyste Close. He had no right. Legal husband or not he shouldn't be there. She'd like the downstairs lot out, all of them. Jordan should by paying proper maintenance through the courts, leave Ruth quite alone. His presence might be disturbing Logan from getting messages through. The brothers weren't in sympathy. While any Cashes remained in Fyst Close Ruth would go on brooding. Ruth needed a real protector, such as herself. Send all Cashes packing, then she could move in. Her brown mog could deal with any rats. She could conduct seances there. Her kitchen failed to attract the proper kind of client. That garage and that garden would make a perfect setting. An autistic child could be trained usefully. Appropriately gowned, those arms could flutter from behind curtains. The Doge could press a button and Rule Britannia! Clients would be moved to ecstasy to see them waving whitely from the other side. Fyste Close was ideal. Those old buildings, refurbished, properly managed, could be a little goldmine. Alive with hauntings, very probably. Had Ruth seen or heard anything of Leslie Ackers? The terrible drowning must have upset him. Had Ruth known the market child, poor sad little thing, was Leslie's sister?

Ruth said she tried not to think of anybody in the past. She wished she had the energy to pack up and leave. She wished she could take Tange away, to find a job, another man, another home. She hadn't been caressed for years, felt dried up as an old leaf. The sad thing was she didn't care. She hadn't bathed for weeks.

'My one, be patient. Wait for the hospital letter. Here, open wide. These will be beneficial.' The Indian's knowledge of herbal medicines was unequalled.

In September a letter came. Tangerine was to come the following day. A list of clothing was included. An early frost silvered the grass where Tangerine was under the pear tree. If it wasn't wet Pearl dumped her there as soon as she was dressed, before joining the garage lot. The garden was so safe. Ruth went to her. She was picking and pulling at something, her hands moving jerkily. By her knees were torn little white scraps. She held the body of the butterfly, was picking the legs and the antennae off.

'Don't, Tange, don't harm it. What has it done to you? It's helpless, don't.'

She led her from the garden up the stairs leading to the bathroom. Logan had built the stairs. Their feet clicked on the metal. Her own child had a nameable disease, was going to be cared for. Saddest of all was knowing that your present malady was the shadowed past, like an echo you couldn't escape.

127

13

SOON after Tangerine went into hospital Pearl came in drunk. Ruth heard her singing in the early hours, heard her stepping the cobble-stones with exaggerated care. 'I Saw Three Ships Go Sailing By, Sailing By'. She'd been dreaming of the garden lady again. She'd been trying to teach Ruth the violin, a surprise for when her mother came at Christmas.

Pearl had a key, stumbling up the stairway, coming into the bed-room, leaning tearfully over her, breathing brandy fumes. Her eyes, unfocused, squashed jellies in her head, showed in the light from the Close. 'Remember, Ruth, I tried. I tried to make things better. Don't be pushed around. Grab life.'

Jordan heard her, turned over, pulled the blankets closer. Nothing to do with him. He dreamed of Primrose who was so nice.

Later, Mrs. Copper took one look at her, lit her cigarette, placed it in her shrinking mouth, told her that she missed the tiddler. Too much strain, she understood. Pearl must come on back to Paddington. Get away for a spell, get away from memories, not to mention all those market nigs, making their row at the back.

'My grandkiddy, my grandkiddy,' wailed Pearl, reaching under the divan, feeling the need again, farting as she bent.

'Poor little Arab. Never mind.'

'She isn't christened. I tried, I tried to make Ruth,' Pearl said with lolling head.

Mrs. Copper said wait till she got back to Paddington, tiddlers there in plenty, winners every one, all waiting for her. And Old Copper, layabout though he might be, was not unfriendly, even if he did lay out with his fists sometimes. Her tiddlers would do the trick. Pearl could have a turn at the toothbrush, too, they could all splash to their hearts' content.

Pearl explained, as Mrs. Copper guided her over the cobblestones, that her grandkiddy's trouble was that she was automatic.

'I agree,' nodded Mrs. Copper. Give the poor soul her head a bit, she'd calm down.

Two letters arrived. Ruh took them down to Jordan, who was typing an outline of his career, to have ready for his book jacket when the publisher asked. He'd found some photographs to sort through. Condensing his biography was fascinating. He was annoyed with Mrs. Copper who should have left Pearl to recover from her orgy, to come down later to him. He missed them, silly though they were. He would miss the food on the tin tray. Primrose was late. He felt a quiet satisfaction that Tangerine was gone, had been led away by Ruth. He sorted his pictures, waiting patiently for Primrose.

'What is it?' He was angry to be disturbed.

'Two letters. You're alone? No Primrose?'

'It's obvious, isn't it?' He hated being alone now, he'd come to rely on his audience. The cockneys helped in spite of not listening to him, whispering about Bingo and other domestic things. Primrose was inspiring, her eyes, her large wet mouth that widened with the wonder of his words, her murmured 'Brilliant, quite, quite brilliant' rounding off each page. How dare those two go off to Paddington, preferring a household of children, cultural dearth to what he offered them? Now Ruth stood waving letters. 'What is it?'

'You ought to see them.' She shivered, though the room was warm. Nothing was left now of Logan except the figure in the corner. Logan's dedication, concentrated aim at truth, was replaced by a roll-topped desk, a pot of unused pencils, some reference books. Jordan didn't use the electric typewriter. Primrose would get his work professionally typed. Her chair was drawn up by the unused reference books. She'd bought an electric kettle.

Ruth put the letters on his desk, avoiding touching him. She had more contact with strangers on buses than with her husband.

'Dear Mr. and Mrs. Cash. For some time conversion of the market and surrounding area has been under consideration. Fyste Close has been bought by Messrs. Podd & Nassatung who have instructed us to act on their behalf. Demolition work will start within the next fortnight. As owner occupier of No. 3 we are prepared to make you a generous purchase offer for the premises. We look forward to completing the formalities as soon as possible and take this opportunity to mention that there are a limited number of shares available in the newly-formed company for sale at an attractive price. We would also mention that should you invest in the company you would be eligible for one or more of the proposed new flats due to be erected. Hoping to hear from you regarding the purchase and allocation of shares to your name.'

'No, Jordan. Not that one, the other letter.'

'What other? What is this? I can't move. Where can I go? I can't move now.'

'The other letter, Jordan. Read that first.'

'What, this? From the hospital? What do they want?' She actually appeared to put more importance in a letter from a hospital than eviction. The roof was threatened.

'Read it.'

'Dear Mrs. Cash. I'm sorry that you have not been able to visit Tangerine in hospital. Since her arrival in the Medlar Ward her condition has showed marked improvement. She appears happy, is beginning to relate to the staff and other children. I cannot, however, overstress the importance of contact with the parents, especially in a case such as Tangerine's, where diagnosis is difficult. I believe that warmth, human contact and visits from home will effect further and lasting improvement. Again, I stress the need for her parents to visit her.'

'Is that the specialist who saw her? What's it to do with me? It's nothing, no affair of mine. You took her.'

'But Jordan, we are married. She's your child, too.'

'My child? I've seen nothing of her. My good girl, I was mad to marry you. A madness that I've more than paid for.'

'And you've done damn well out of the arrangement. My money bought the roof. She won't get better without visits. The letter says.'

'Then visit her. Don't bother me about it.'

She blinked. She wouldn't tell him about feeling ill, wouldn't appeal to his sympathy. He had none for her. She'd eaten quantities of the Doge's pills to combat the pain of failure. The failing as a wife, as mother, the failure of her existence in Fyste Close. They had a delaying effect, a first priority came last, you delayed action, sleep was the prime necessity. Love, obligations, receded with the pills. The letter jerked her, reality must be faced.

'I intend to go. I should have gone before. The thing of it is,

Jordan, we needn't go together, but she needs us. I must go.'

'Go then. Don't think I will. I won't.' He'd been quite sufficiently put out by both of them. He was a burdened man. Let her go where she wanted.

He still expected her to walk meekly, dismissing her with Henry VIII hating eyes. His unkempt appearance soon went when he got other women round him.

'Damn you. What have you ever done for us?'

'You're noisy. Your mother disturbed me with her brawling. My output has suffered.' He was even more disturbed by Pearl's defection than her midnight wails. Mrs. Copper was treacherous, stealing her away to Paddington.

'You've done well for yourself financially.'

'I've paid. You've had my contributions.'

'What contributions?'

'What I gave Pearl for you each week. Three pounds fifty.'

Ruth said nothing. Pearl couldn't help herself. Weak, straining towards Jesus or her bottle in desperate appeal, no longer bothering to dye her hair, she was beyond help. Weakness left uncauterized got worse. Ruth would contact Dr. Greanbach for advice. She must face the problem.

'She's a thief. My work has suffered.' He tried, he'd done his best, had tried to call her Mother Pearl to please her, in recognition for her trays. She'd repaid him by drinking noisily at night before dashing off to Paddington to pray over some Coppers half-way through his reading of 'No More'. Primrose's wet mouth shaping 'brilliant' was inestimable; he'd like the other two as well. Ruth had no right to upset him with hospital letters. He couldn't wait to tell Primrose. Ruth had no right to bother him at all. The other letter, the offer of cheap shares in a profitable concern, was a different matter. But what about his study? He mustn't be homeless, not again, not at this turning point. 'No more', was almost finished. Next week Primrose would be getting it typed. Then presto, the world would be astonished. Primrose rose to any emergency. Given a reasonable sum for the premises he could cut loose permanently from Ruth, as Gauguin had intended, forget his past insanity of choice, forget he'd ever called her Ragged Ruth, his own true secretary.

'You know what I think about your damned writing. What about Logan's work.' Jordan had ignored the man from Mayfair who wanted to exhibit his sculpture, ignored his viewpoint. Contemporary sculpture had lost an important contributor. If they moved what would happen to the garden?

'It's nothing to do with me.' Jordan forced back a mouthful of bile. His stomach heaved, a reminder of the time he'd left the library. This time he'd be prudent, plan escape without a hitch. The letter was the key, the letter from the firm of Podd & Nassatung. He told her quietly that he'd look into the matter, leave it to him. He'd see to it, sign relevant papers, leave Podd & Nassatung to him. She could attend to the hospital in any way she saw fit.

She took the hospital letter. The only smell in the garage now was the flex of Primrose's kettle, a burning rubber smell. The smells of cold steel, linseed, and diesel oil, of putty, woodshavings and rope were gone.

At the mouth of the Close the Doge stood, leaning her face into Leslie Acker's smirking one. Her bun made her look crazy. 'My one, I have been feeling vibrations. I knew you'd come. Your sad little sister needs companionship. I have a plan'. When she saw Ruth she called to her. 'Ah my other one, how is your Gingernut? Don't let her forget her Aunt.'

Leslie walked away. The sight had no effect on Ruth. He was in the past. Nothing could kill the real Logan, not death, or plottings, time couldn't destroy his work. Leslie was incidental. She rang the hospital.

The receptionist was reluctant. Dr. Greanbach was a busy man. Those wanting parley must make appointments, not waste his time jabbering into the telephone. She had a letter, why didn't she answer it?

'You see, Dr. Greanbach, the Close is coming down. We had a letter. Can Tange come home?'

'Demolished, do you mean? Where will you go? She is vastly improved, vastly, but not ready to return yet. I don't recommend it. What will you do?' He tried to keep his tones unruffled, not to show anxiety. Tangerine mustn't leave, not until she was ready. Despite the chronic shortage of beds, she must stay. Accommodation, beds, always the same, not enough. The main frustration of urban society was accommodation. A roof, a bed somewhere, a place to be ill, to recuperate, to fail or prosper. Homes were split, families disunited, lacking the requirement. Always the same, never enough. And outside, children waited. Beyond his telephone and desk, beyond his couch and instrument trolley, beyond the grouped doll families, were children waiting. They waited by his door. They tapped their plaster casts. They knocked uncontrollable limbs about their faces sick and shrieking. His appointment book was full. Tangerine didn't need institutionalising. One of the luckier ones. And Mrs. Cash had failed to visit her. She had another home planned already, yes?

'I want her back. A weekend perhaps. In case we move soon. I want her badly. I want her to remember home as it was.' To remember the garden, Logan's work. The love would linger in her unconscious mind, Logan's love, the close times, times of love, of care and gaiety. Before Pearl came on the scene, before Jordan reappeared. Would she be stuck with Jordan until she'd been through the divorce courts?

'I have to put her well-being before anything. How are you in yourself?'

'Better. Much, much better. I realise I've lived wrongly. Too cut off. I've been looking through my diaries. It's obviously been wrong.'

'Diaries? Have you always kept diaries?'

'Since I could first write. Is Tange really better?'

'Go to the Medlar. See for yourself.'

Ruth asked if she still waved her arms about, if she rocked, played with the glove, spun without purpose on her toes. She hoped she hadn't bitten any nurses. She pictured them holding bloodied hankies to their hands, concealing annoyance. He said she'd stopped her mannerisms as soon as she got to the Medlar Ward. She was speaking, slowly, admittedly, but speaking sentences. She could sing the plaintive carol that he'd heard her whistle. Mrs. Cash taught her the song, yes? Outwardly she was a normal child. He wished that Mrs. Cash and others like her could accept the need of unconditional love, of love outwardly expressed, regardless of a child's behaviour. On her bed chart he'd written 'Tangerine needs extra loving'. It often worked. Illness, unacceptable conduct, deviation from the normal, often sprang from lack of attentive love. He prescribed no drugs. He spoke quickly into the receiver, delaying the treament of the tapping, crying ones outside. Tangerine could go home for a trial weekend. It was lamentable that they were moving. The main secret, the talisman, was love. Meanwhile could he see her diaries? Had she really never missed a day's entry?

She told him they had been her lifeline through the long sad years. She told the diary about Tange, about Pearl's awfulness, how isolated she'd been. After re-reading them she realised the pattern. Isolation acquired in childhood soon became habit. At school the girls disliked her for preferring the boys secretly behind the bicycle sheds, secret meetings, never twice with the same boy, never mixing with the playground lot. They talked about her, called her names. Her job was a continuation of the earlier acquired state, not mixing, remote, on a pedestal and talked about. Hatred of her boozing mother, her reluctant dependence on a worried father, led to weak relationships later. Logan had showed her what real love was. The others, the groping schoolboys, students, pick-ups in clubs, were names in her diary. Over the years they totalled unacceptably, any stop-gap did when you were lonely. Bodies in the dark were much alike. The calculated capturing, the whispered sweetnesses. An hour, a week, six weeks, rarely longer before the termination and fresh chase. 'I love you darling'. The pain and the excitement of a new affair, the shock of ending, though you knew it was inevitable. The astonished pain, assuaged by the inimical desire for new love. Dr. Greanbach would read these things. Would he understand that the nick-name 'Art School Bike' had been earned in childhood years before they said it? She asked him why he really wanted the diaries.

He said that Tangerine's signs of autism particularly interested him. The field was a neglected one. So little was known, there was a need for research. The more he could find out about the background the better. Grandparents, parents, no detail was extraneous. The wartime hardship of her grandmother, evacuated, parents bombed, then Ruth herself being fostered as a child, were possibly more than curious chance. The diary might well be a goldmine of information. Would she help him?

'All right, if you can read my writing.' Packed into bean boxes under the divan, she'd bring them, piles of them, the thumbed exercise books printed in pencil at four, bound volumes later, 'Pet Lovers Diary', 'Teenage Diary', 'Diary for 18 and Over'. She still wrote childishly. She'd bring them with her when she came for Tangerine.

He put his receiver down. He heard the tapping and the wailing of the sick outside with a feeling of refreshed energy. His lucky day. Like many neurotics, Mrs. Cash had reserves of strength, untapped as yet. Her help would be invaluable. He must check with her about those herbal remedies. A mistake to dabble with quacks. A weekend at home with her mother might show something more about the fascinating Cash child, show something more about autism.

Tangerine refused to hold Ruth's hand. She skipped. She was as light as flame. The frosty air in the market smelled nice. There was Aunt's large brown cat. Big. Big as a lion. Skip your knees high, white knees, higher. There were black people near, at the back, out there. They came at night. At night you couldn't see their faces but you heard them. They walked about. They played their tunes, up and down. You didn't tell your mother, sleeping heavily from Aunt's pills. 'One Could Whistle And One Could Sing, One Could Play The Violin'. You wanted to be home again. There was something there you missed. Something important. The nurses were kind, they played, they gave you toys. You wanted to be home.

Ruth hurried to keep up with her. Now she had a child like everyone else's. Thanks to Dr. Greanbach and the Medlar Ward she had a talented beauty skipping ahead with a sweet high voice. He might find somewhere for them, somewhere to live. She'd like to help his work, looked forward to it. She could type out the diaries for him if he wanted. She was so grateful to him, looked forward to working with that kind wise face near.

The Doge beckoned from her upper window, waving her spoon. A little myrrh in the mince made it toothsome.

She wouldn't keep them, she had important business, just wanted to welcome them. Her table was covered with papers. The Gingernut was well and kicking? Here, have a dip. Have some of Aunt's nice black sweets.

Before they left the Doge, Ruth bought some candles from her to decorate the kitchen table, make it festive. She would read to her later, like other mothers with other normal children. They

135

wouldn't go in the garden yet, or near the garage, straight upstairs.

She sensed someone had been there. The divan was pulled from the wall. She sensed someone had been harmful. She stood holding the candles. The divan was pulled and left crooked. The valance was pulled up. Her diaries were gone, the cardboard box containers closed with string had been taken away. The box with the spare parts of the inflatable doll had been taken. There was an empty brandy bottle, one that had contained aspirins and the old typewriter. She told Tangerine to go to the bathroom, to fill the wash-basin and wash. She'd straighten, light her candles first. Go, Tangerine. She heard her turn the tap as she smelled the smoke. She heard the crackling of light objects burning. Smoke rose outside the bathroom window.

'Smoke. Smoke, look', Tangerine said happily, splashing her hands. Sparks flew up, grey tatters of ash rising in the air, fluttering outside the window. They heard the laughing through the glass.

Jordan and Primrose stood throwing her diaries into the bonfire in the garden. With one hand Primrose nursed the box containing the spare parts of her doll, with the other she threw in the books one by one. She was giggling. She was content.

'The quicker they're disposed of the better', he said. The fire was burning well. Fire cleansed. Fire purged. He had no qualms now. His stomach felt comfortable. The past was over, wouldn't trouble him again. He'd done his deal with the solicitor, had made sure of the legalities. All trace of Ruth must be extinguished. He had Primrose.

Only Tangerine saw the little face looking over the wall, vacant, slitty-eyed, heard the feet scampering. 'Smoke, smoke', she said, splashing the water about. As the fire died the ashes whitened like snowflakes.

14

THE Doge felt calm. She sank her teeth into another bootlace, her jawbone moving in a circular motion before each gulp. She swallowed her blackened saliva with a sense of achievement. She had got her way. She walked with the immortals at last. Her plan with the Indian had borne fruit. The Indian had been occupied throughout his life with business ventures; it was her first foray into anything more adventurous than oddments and jobments. The life of a spiritual palmist was precarious. Now she was entering a new cycle, a change of karma. It was beyond her dreams, a partnership with the Indian. That they'd never even met made it more spell-binding. Not that she'd abandon her meetings; she'd keep in touch with the occult. She still believed that Logan, who must be out of Summerland now, would get through with a message. Now, she and the Indian would tackle the more important field of property de-velopment. With inflation going rampant now was the time. As usual their arrangements had been made by post. The little market brat, Leslie's sister, had been so useful, running messages back and forth. The Doge had relied on her for years. That she couldn't speak was an advantage: reliable little post-brat. Because of these time-taking activities, letter-writing, the signing of documents, she'd been obliged to invent a simplified method of palmistry. Instead of palms she read the backs of hands. With less wrinkles to confuse her she could work twice as fast. 'Over, please. Back of the hand,' she told them sharply. After the first surprise of it her clients didn't mind having their four raised metacarpals peered at. It made a change. Love, money, love and death, a bit of health, some travel, that's what they expected. Don't trust the dark man, love the fair, you'll have a lot of brats. Chance of romance late in life, you'll pass water before crossing it. Believe, believe. They swallowed all of it. Once she'd read the back of the hand of an old woman in her glove, had said she'd bear eight brats, win a contest, Miss Great

Britain. Only when the glove was dipping into the woman's purse did the Doge notice. Glove or skin, what did it matter if they paid? Since the Doge's alliance with the Indian she sneezed a lot more. Her chest hurt, a hurting that her gooseberry puffs failed to alleviate. Once she'd moved into Fyste Close it would stop . . . She'd wanted to get into the garage for years. The Indian had solved it. They'd buy the Cashes out. He had plans for Fyste Close. It had been simple to concoct a letter from a make-believe solicitor, with the help of the Indian's clever printing press. So the firm of Podd & Nassatung was born. Soon she'd be sitting by that garden reading backs of hands. Jordan and those three creatures would be gone. Hands revealed a lot. The Indian dipped his clever brown-skinned ones into many a pie. Work permits, passports, accommodation for his countrymen, bailing the unfortunate from jail, anything at all to do with printing. And his oils and baccy. His poppy pills were very strong indeed. She imagined his face, teak-brown, old as a withered leaf, lined from compassionate service to his kinsfolk who flitted in and out of his alley way. Guru Nassatung was their saviour. It was his influence that gave the Doge an instant interest in Ruth, her Indiany type of clothing, her jewelry. The sad little post-brat sister had let her brother Leslie know about Ruth and Logan going to Battersea, had run with a note to tell. It was a disastrous day. You couldn't go against the tragic hand of fate, nor could you alter human nature. Leslie was bitter. Rejection soured people. The Indian understood, he was a gentleman who knew many ways of lifting and lowering the spirits. Backs of hands and spiritual meetings would be her Fyste Close specialities. The purchase went through easily. Fear of eviction made Jordan sign for a nice low price. Wisely, the Indian looked ahead.

Fyste Close wasn't coming down yet. The only immediate change would be at No. 3. One day the other buildings would be converted into offices, that was where money was, in the offices of industry and commerce. The Indian wouldn't let the old buildings remain vacant. He had the protection of his kinsfolk to consider. Eventually the Doge hoped to be looking at her backs of hands in the light of neon strips. Instead of rats and Indian pipes the Close would ring with the clicking, ringing, rattling of computerised machines, telexes and the like. Ruth could live on quietly upstairs while she and the Indian cleaned up a packet. The Doge had often dreamed that Ruth was her own daughter. Her dream would flower, her skinny lovely one in Indiany clothes would be hers, upstairs. The blood mother, that Pearl person, was best off with the Coppers. She'd be happy there, kept out of the picture busy baptising those brats. You got to know who would chum up with who, Pearl and the Copper person were made for each other. A lover of the brandy bottle, she'd be no loss, had never properly been a mother. The Doge blessed the poppy pills, the Indian's expertise. What she did not want was the recovery of the Gingernut. She'd not reckoned with the doctor. Dr. Greanbach was formidable. The Gingernut must stay ailing. She had plans to put the sad little post-brat, sister of Leslie, with the Gingernut, arms linked. The two could wave together at a sign. With the Ginge compos mentis this would be less easy. No, it wouldn't do for the Greanbach cure to work. She wanted them like twins, two helpful ectoplasmic sightings, two lots of waving arms. Buttons, dolls, smoke, poppy pills didn't thwart the doctor. At the time of Ruth's pregnancy the Indian had written Doge a note. 'Believe, believe, a dolly can be powerful.' Her crystal ball had glistened prettily that Christmas.

'Well, Puss, stop sulking.' She would feed him before going to see Ruth, explain to her. She needn't move at all. She could stay peacefully in her own quarters. She gathered up some more poppy pills excitedly. The name of the firm was wonderful. Jordan had bought shares too, after selling No. 3 at a friendship price. Perhaps he might interest Peter Pownde-Welling, make the firm into a Consortium. 'Podd, Nassatung & Pownde'. She snatched another bootlace. 'Myrrh is mine, its bitter perfume, breathes a life of gathering gloom, sorrowing, sighing, bleeding, dying, sealed in a stone cold tomb.' Poor little Indiany Ruth. She'd had to do it, had to show Jordan and Primrose the place. Diaries, records of times past, were better burned to ash. She'd only stood and pointed, there, there under the divan. Out. Burn. Unhealthy. The lines that counted most in life were written on the hands, not written by them in a book. Primrose and Jordan were in Weybridge with the bits of the clever doll.

'My one, my one, what happened? Hubby left you?' His garage door was open, his desk cleared of his important books and his electrical typing machine. His lovely shiny kettle was a loss. The only familiar object was the er . . . creation in the corner. The pieces in the garden were still there, spoiling it.

'He left. With Primrose. They burned my diaries, Doge.' Ruth stared at her. She couldn't expect her to understand the enormity of it. Unless you kept a diary yourself, nobody could understand.

'Poor one. I understand. Tell me.'

Ruth had threatened Primrose with the police. She'd shouted. Damn them. Damn them to hell. Damn them. She'd run down the metal outside stairs with Tangerine, had felt her trembling . . . The bonfire was still glowing in the heart of it, the ashes greying, whitening. Primrose's chinchilla coat quivered in the heat. Jordan's beard moved up and down, blustering that if Primrose went he would. She led the way, a queen with him behind, having taken the doll bits from her. She smiled so gaily, triumphantly. Could childlessness bring out such evil?

'My one, take one.' The poppy pills could calm, a few would be effective.

'No, Doge. I'm taking nothing.' She must stay calm and wise. She had to move. She had to fend for herself. She had to find a home, a place of safety for Tangerine. Now it was goodbye for keeps to Jordan who had treated valuable research as junk, had discarded her life's experience. The metal steps squeaked under Primrose's weight as she went upwards. Jordan looked back from the third step, sneering at her for the last time. She'd done it once to him, belittled, scorned his work, remember? Perhaps she knew now how it felt, but whether she did or not, it was nothing to do with him. He'd paid his price.

Tangerine had started fluttering her hands as she had before she went into the Medlar. Ruth had held her close, not looking at the dying fire. She must stay calm.

'Good news, my one. The Indian has set up a Consortium. He has bought the Close. You don't have to worry.' The wise brown one had saved their bacon. Her spiritual mate in present time, Ruth would become their spiritual daughter. The Consortium would bring all this about. She sensed that her Genoese of yesteryear would bless the present union. It was most fortunate that Jordan had left without bother, another happy mating. Primrose and he would flourish in Weybridge, while Peter laboured at his healing. Ruth should never have involved herself with the progeny of undertakers. Unless that gingernut stayed autistic she'd be of little use in the garage.

'But Jordan told me. The letter came from a solicitor. Official.'

'Yes, yes. The Indian. The Indian has arranged everything.' No need to mention her own co-partnership, not yet. Hubby had gone, that was the important thing. The Doge licked her stained upper lip, before another sneeze.

'Jordan said I must be out.' Out, out and all her diaries gone, nothing to show, nothing left of the long sad years. His undertaking hands had seen to disposal.

'Lies. Lies, all lies.' The Indian would protect Ruth, Fyste Close and the whole market. There were no limits to his power. He was inviolate. She was in partnership with deity.

'But will it come down?'

'Not yet. Not yet.' With the undertaking brothers, the three interfering women, encumbrances all out of the light of Fyste Close they'd have true peace. Just Ruth and her.

'When?'

'Nothing is yet settled, not for Fyste Close at any rate.' She believed that work would start in the next street, over the back, very soon. Rule Britannia. She'd even found a little playmate for the Ginge.

'Who? What playmate?' It would take more than a playmate to restore Tange after the shock of the bonfire, the shouting and the leaving. She'd taken her upstairs, had warmed her, rocked, kissed, sung to her, had tried to still her hands. Then they had gone down to the empty garage to see 'Fruition', walking round it gravely, before feeling, touching it as Logan had intended. There were no other children, who did the Doge intend? There were some Indian children, unfriendly, recently arrived, not speaking English, keeping to themselves.

'My one, she is er ... known to you. Leslie's young sister. You remember her?'

'His sister? That monstrosity in the hood? That ... fiend?' That insensate face with soulless eyes. The red fists hitting her. There at the beginning, there at the end, at Logan's end. Malefic. Fiend.

'My one, there is no real harm. Sad little thing. A lone one. She's not grown, not developed.' In her own sad little way the post-brat might be autistic. Of equal height the two could help each other, play games and sing. The sad little brat might steal a smile from the Gingernut.

'She is evil.'

'Not too evil, just a little. Sad.' She'd always been like that, mute, backward, sad. Happy were they who stayed underdeveloped, those having no wish for betterment. They could play while Ruth got on with the typing. The Doge fancied her hand at a bit of writing. 'Backs Of Hands' by Lady Podesta Doge. The Indian would print it, after Ruth had prepared it on her typewriter. Ruth would soon stop brooding, she'd be so busy typing. You must accept Fate's hand. Unalterable. She'd get on with 'Backs Of Hands' while the sad ones played in the garden. She'd get on with teaching them to wave at meetings. Ruth could keep the er . . . creation now. What luck. Here, have a bootlace.

'I don't want that creature near Tangerine. Fiend.' The market girl had marked their lives, couldn't the Doge understand that?

'Believe, my one. Trust in the mystic influences.' The sad brat was rejected, why not accept her? Next weekend did Ruth say? The Ginge was coming home again the following weekend? She left a handful of poppy pills behind her. She'd have her name put over the garage door. The two little brats would love their Aunt Pod. Literature, spiritual palmistry and meetings would flourish at No. 3. She would keep her Emporium, her own brainchild. Oils, wheeling and dealing, oddments, jobments would be relaxation from the strain of seances, spiritual backs of hands and authorship. The Emporium and the Consortium would govern the whole market. Brown-skinned ones loved occultism. She debated the possibility of getting Dr. Greanbach financially involved, winning him over to her point of view. That Medlar Ward was not the place for Ginge. Vibrations never lied. The Doge had been right not to underestimate the power of buttons. She thought with warmth again of the Indian and his wise writing. A dolly was a powerful thing.

'Dr. Greanbach asked me for my help. I want to. My experience with Tange could prove an important link in his research into autism.'

'No doubt, no doubt. She's coming next weekend then?'

'Yes.' She wouldn't throw her hand in, give up because of the loss

142

of the diaries, she would help him all she could. She'd write what she could from memory. Tangerine would regain the progress lost by the weekend trouble. Much could be done for the condition, particularly when taken early. Remedial teaching, devoted care and Montessori equipment worked wonders. She'd devote all her time to helping Dr. Greanbach, help him to find out more about a disease that rendered children incapable of sociable reaction. But why her? What had she done to be afflicted with a child with an obscure disease?

The Doge supposed a letter to the hospital would find Dr. Greanbach, it was worth a try. Meanwhile she had an inspiration. The er ...creation might be useful as an ancillary piece of equipment. It could be wired to light up movingly in signals. Two letters then, one to the doctor, one to the Indian, to let him know that Gingernut would be home in Fyste Close the following weekend. His kinsmen always worked on Sundays. Demolition work on Rolling Row could start directly. The Row backed onto Fyste Close. The Indian's kinsmen would appear. Smilingly, they'd pull down those old houses. With robes tucked into overalls their dark hands would see to the matter with minimum disturbance. The Doge said nothing to Ruth. There was no point in the Ginge getting alarmed ahead of time. A small fright, some tumbling houses, would work wonders. Her head felt starry. How good the Indian was, providing work for his kinsmen and compatriots, bettering the world. Rolling Row might be a supermarket, or a brats' play-centre with flyover. Podd, Nassatung & Pownde would expand, there'd be no stopping the progress. The Ginge must have a little fright. It was necessary.

'If I can stay here it will save a lot of worry, Doge.' As well as helping with the research she could exhibit Logan's work, a permanent show in the garage. There'd be no entrance fee. All art lovers could come in, stroll round, enjoy it. Eventually she might write something herself about autism, something, some work in her own right.

'Yes yes.' The Doge strode angrily away. Ruth would soon settle. She was puzzled about the cracking of the distorting mirror in her shop. Work started on schedule. The machinery moved in. Bulldozers, a claw-crane, a crusher ball for extra stubborn walls. The brown ones went to work with picks and mallets first, having removed the slates from roofs. They kicked out windows with their strong dark feet.

Demolishing, destroying what had been put up by a society that treated them unkindly, appealed to them. Their turn had come. The work made their teeth flash in their brown faces. Retaliation at last against a people who had made them unwelcome. Guru Nassatung had saved them with his cunning and his money. For him they worked with zeal, rigging the crusher ball in excess of energy. It made a lovely crashing, filling the air with sound, though it wasn't necessary on such weak low walls. The noise of the picks, mallets and the thudding crusher beat rhythmically as they chattered. Punjabi, Tamil, Hindustani mixed with laughing rang round Rolling Row. Raze it. Knock it down. The air was filled with dust, snow-white and grey, falling about, falling into Fyste Close. Dark hands pushed levers, buttons. A turbaned head bobbed through a gap in the brickwork. The rubble-picker swung over, opening its clawed teeth to scoop up masonry. The driver laughed.

He wasn't blamed. The coroner said no one could be blamed. Unfortunate. Death by misadventure. It was unfortunate that a brick from the back wall, weakened by vibrations and previous cracking, fell onto the head of a little girl playing in a garden in Fyste Close. Tangerine Cash died instantly while playing under the pear trees with Eustacia Ackers, her little friend.

The tapping of Ruth's typewriter sounded early and late in Fyste Close. It was said that the Indian mourned Tangerine as he inspected the market from behind the darkened glass windows of the purple Rolls.

144